SHELTER MY

I0671427

HEART

MariaLisa deMora

Photography: Invicta Photography

Model: James Clippinger

Edited by Hot Tree Editing

Cover design: Debera Kuntz

First Published 2018

ISBN 13: 978-1-946738-25-7

DEDICATION

For Jacqueline Carey, who taught so many of
us the true meaning behind the phrase,
"Love as thou wilt."

Contents

ACKNOWLEDGMENTS

I've learned that when a character raises their hand in mid-sentence, so to speak, it's the perfect time to listen.

In only five days Lewis, Po'Boy of our dreams, fed me this story and I took it and ran with it. Yay for listening to my gut, because this little story feels pretty special.

I wrapped it up on Oct. 11, 2018, which is Coming Out Day. While these characters have already come out to their close friends, they're beginning to learn that for folks who don't follow the hetero path, every day can be coming out day. Dealing with that, and the innate insecurities that often surface during any building relationship, and adding in the needs of three individual partners, and we've got the start of a complex story.

I hope you enjoy this tiny window into their lives.

Woofully yours,

~ML

Chapter One

Lewis

Ralph Lewis sat and stared out the window, one hand holding a beer the chill had long since fled from. He inched his ass towards the edge of the upholstered armchair and leaned back, head cradled against the back cushion. From here, he could understand Crissy's attachment to their screened-in back porch, the chair positioned where she could watch the sun rising over the delta. It made his belly warm to think about taking care of her, this house being part of his care, his responsibility. She deserved all that and so much more.

Ankle propped across one knee, he dangled the bottle loosely from his fingers, swinging it gently back

1

and forth like a metronome. Thirty minutes later saw him adjusting positions, two empties placed near the chair creating a quiet clinking as his foot brushed against them. He drained the bottle he held, followed with a soft, "Shit," grimacing slightly at the bitterness of the now-warm beer.

Sleep hadn't found him tonight, stranding him high and dry on the sands of frustration and fear. Things were in motion in his club, the Incoherent MC, and he wasn't certain how to slide past the snap of a trap he'd set himself. Twisted, his national president, had called yesterday with a demand for a chat, and Lewis knew the man wouldn't be pleased with what Lewis had to say, or what he intended as the final outcome. *I just gotta find a way to survive his wrath*. It might be past time for what was coming, but change came hard to an organization so steeped in tradition.

"That's a brown study, Po'Boy. You comin' back inside anytime soon?"

That rough, deep voice carried a broad river of affection and the tiniest hint of frustration. Lewis, otherwise known as Po'Boy, twisted his neck to look towards the sliding doors that led from the porch back into the house proper. He smiled at the man standing there, one bare foot still inside the threshold as if he were uncertain of his welcome. Low-slung jeans completed his wardrobe, probably plucked from the bedroom floor when Ty decided to come looking for him.

"Hey, baby." Ty's eyes warmed, and Lewis liked to see it, evidence of how much Ty liked it whenever Lewis used a sweet name for his lover. The stress-etched lines in his face softened, corners of his lips curling up just the slightest amount. Lewis told him, "Ain't studyin' nothin' in particular. I'm just sittin'."

"You've been 'just sitting' all night." Tyler Sawyer narrowed his eyes, clearly finding Lewis' words suspicious. He was the other part of the equation that had sent Lewis to the porch. Not an intentional banishment from their bed, and if Ty even imagined Lewis felt that way at all, he'd be falling over himself to apologize for whatever slight Lewis had dreamed up.

Tonight, it hadn't been Ty or Crissy that caused the ripples through Lewis' head. No, that was all himself.

The two of them were in a relationship, equal partners, with Crissy Emmerson forming the third leg of their triad. Something they all had to work at, because not only were they still fairly new together, their road had not been bump free. On the surface, everything looked good, mostly because it *was* good. *So fucking good*. But the things that had broken them before still were in play, and until Lewis knew without a doubt that Ty could have what he needed in his own club, the Caddo Hobos, he'd be on edge and fighting to keep both Ty and Crissy in his life.

"Liar." Ty—also called Wrench for his sharply honed ability to become whatever tool his motorcycle club needed to wield—had some experience reading people, a skill Lewis found irritating when turned against him as it was now. Ty challenged him further by stalking the final strides to where he sat. Lewis didn't rise, didn't change position in response, so when the man finally pulled to a stop inches away, he was left facing one of his favorite parts of Ty's anatomy.

Lewis reached up, dragging his blunt nails crossways along the fabric of Ty's jeans, chuckling deep in his chest when the cock hiding under that fabric gave a visible twitch to accompany the raking touch. *This is mine.* "What if I said I was thinking about this?" As he spoke, he continued his firm caress along the tightening crotch of Ty's pants. He leaned forwards, putting his foot flat on the floor to brace himself. Mouth beside his hand, he traced the outline of a clearly visible erection with his lips, blowing hot air across every inch.

It didn't take long to pull a response from Ty. Voice hoarse, he gasped out, "Ah, God. You fucking asshole."

Ty's reaction prompted him to take it further. "I am all of that," he allowed. *But I'm not lying.* He placed the empty bottle next to the others on the floor. With both hands now free, he molded the fabric to Ty's member, outlining the length of his cock, touch lingering longest where he could tease the head. As soon as he unbuttoned, unzipped, and tugged the jeans down, he mouthed the rigid erection, flicking his tongue along the underside for a moment before slipping the fat crown between his lips, each step of the way bringing curses to Ty's lips, protestations all tangled up in demands for more, until Lewis was confident he was twisting Ty inside out.

He wasn't lying. He had been thinking of Ty's cock, but where he'd been thinking about putting it was a completely different hole. His mind had been a movie screen, images looped and playing all the ways he could make Ty lose his mind with his touch, his mouth. *And my cock*. But, he'd also been worrying over the one time he'd had Ty on his knees, turning it around and round in his head, studying every action, every word he could remember, trying to dissect it. That had been a dark day, a moment their connection seemed on the brink of disaster. He could still visualize the moment when Ty had fully realized what their bond could cost him. The man hadn't just backed away, he'd fled as if his life depended on it.

Understanding what had driven him to run, Lewis had let him go, because the same demons had also chased him forever. At the time, the break seemed a natural devolving, where the club won because it had to. The club was everything, and they were just members, cogs in the wheel. But God, it had cost all of them. So much.

Don't wanna think about that anymore. Thinking about it too long would have him pulling back again, making the wrong decisions, and drive a bigger rift between him and Ty than before.

In an effort to quiet his mind, Lewis took Ty to the back of his throat and held there, controlling his breath and swallowing twice, three times, until Ty finally gave way to instinct and the demands of his body, with a groan and a pump of his hips. Another slow glide, then he pulled out as Lewis gasped for breath. He offered his mouth again and, in a heartbeat, Ty was thrusting forwards, strong fingers reaching down to encircle Lewis' throat. Not constricting, not choking him, just connecting in a way that let him feel how hard Lewis was working to bring his lover pleasure.

"Still—" Ty panted between the words, "a liar."

Lewis pulled off slowly, breathing through his nose as he paused in his retreat to reclaim an inch or two before easing away farther, only to repeat the cycle. *If he can still string words together, I'm doin' it wrong*. He redoubled his efforts, hoping the difference between the heat of his mouth and the cool night air would help keep Ty on edge, give him more time with Ty's dick in his mouth, and more chances to pleasure the man, showing without words how much he meant to Lewis. *Plus, the side benefit is that I do love suckin' cock*. Lapping at the end of the stiff dick with the flat of his tongue, he swirled the tip gently, lashing across the salty slit with a chest-rattling hum of enjoyment. *Might say I'm partial to it, even more so to this cock in particular*. He found air in his lungs to rasp out, "Not lying."

"Fuck, Lewis." Ty's words were rough, voice jagged with his fight for control. "*God*."

Lewis sucked in a series of light pulses, lips firm around Ty's cock before he pulled off again, smirked up at Ty and asked, "What'd you come out here for again?" Without waiting on a response, he engulfed Ty's cock and took it deep, his lover's groan tearing through the air as he forgot his question. His fingers tightened around Lewis' throat possessively again, just how Lewis liked it, taking both of them out of their minds and into the calm place where passion ruled, loving and being loved was paramount, and life would always be good.

Chapter Two

Ty

Lewis' pulse thudded under Ty's touch, and he struggled for control of every breath, beating back the shouts that wanted to pour from him.

From the first time he'd seen that sly smile on Lewis' face, it had worked its way under Ty's skin, amping him up and then tearing the ground out from under him with an attraction that had been terrifying. That same smirk had driven Ty to follow this man into a strange bar, back when they weren't even a possibility. And the damned knowing grin had stopped him in his tracks during an intense breakup scene stupidly instigated by him. That grin meant Ty having his first taste of cock while working to drive the expression from Lewis' features...had ended in disaster.

He still shied away from the memory. Even now, two months later, the wedge he had forced between the three of them burned. The wreckage he'd left behind meant the three of them had suffered in solitude, going through so much upheaval alone.

And it was all my fault.

Crissy and Lewis both said they forgave him for the breakup, but even now, he didn't know if he could forgive himself. And as much as Lewis liked to talk through things, verbally dissecting all the current, and far more pleasant aspects of their relationship at length—at times until Ty and Crissy had been driven to derail his monologue by tackling him into bed—Lewis had never mentioned it again.

He'd talk about anything else, but not that night. His avoidance alone told Ty it was important.

Ty had learned from Crissy that Lewis had gone to her in the aftermath. He knew Lewis had spent the rest of that night in her bed, and together they'd made love, laying down memories she had used to get through the weeks they'd all been apart. Because while it might have been Ty who ran, Lewis hadn't stuck with Crissy, leaving them to go their separate ways. Crissy had lost the connection with them, Lewis had lost the solace he'd found away from the club, and Ty had lost—everything.

He might never really forgive me. Ty stared down at Lewis' upturned face, gliding his fingertips across eyelids fluttering underneath the light touch. *I gotta find a way to fix it*. Needed to rebuild the trust. Sure, he knew Lewis trusted both him and Crissy without question when it came to being faithful. But the way Ty had broken them left a scar of fear deep inside this man he loved. Lewis made that clear every time he shifted away from Ty's touch in bed. Trust was key.

Ty groaned when Lewis wrapped his tongue around the head of his cock. His cheeks hollowed as he drew the full length into his mouth and Ty's brain stuttered, overwhelmed by the heat and pressure. "Jesus fuck." *This right here is why Lewis is so good at keeping the topic at bay*. "You drive me insane." Fingers tugged at his sac, handling him exactly rough enough, the sensual rolling motion riding the welcome edge of pain.

Ty scraped his nails through Lewis' hair, twisting and gripping to hold him in place, dick deep in his throat. His hips jerked forwards, and he gave in to the movement, sliding in and out for a series of shallow, fast strokes, fucking Lewis' mouth. "Love this, Lewis."

Lewis hummed far back in his throat, the vibration upping the peaks of pleasure Ty had beating through his body. He knew Lewis would be happy to do this all day long, would give as much as Ty would take and be happy. But the moment Ty tried to counter with even a touch, he'd bet money Lewis would shut it down fast, redirecting so he was always the one giving, never taking what he needed.

At first, Ty hadn't been certain what was happening. It seemed coincidental that just as he reached for Lewis, the man would slide along Crissy's side and out of reach. A spontaneous movement resulting in a shared, intense focus on their lover. That was how it went down when it would be the three of them in bed, on the couch, or even in the truck riding to town, seated three across the bench seat. Once he could understand, twice he could chalk up to being a fluke, but when it happened again and again, he couldn't ignore the deep-seated problem.

When Ty was alone with the man like this, Lewis managed to always dominate the encounters, deftly steering actions along a pathway that made it easy for Ty to follow. He was the novice, after all, it made sense for him to shadow the lead of the more experienced man. And why not, when it brought them both pleasure?

Last night, Ty received final confirmation of his fears. In bed with Lewis, Crissy working late on a project for an ad client, Ty had found an unwelcome affirmation when he attempted to divert his role into a more active one. He'd kissed Lewis hard, sucked and played with his nipples, and then made his intentions clear as he'd moved farther down the mattress in their bed. Unfortunately for Lewis, Ty hadn't missed the look of near panic that had flashed across his features.

The expression was there and gone in a moment. There was the briefest of pauses, and then Lewis wasted no time in getting things back on track, his hold on Ty's jaw drawing him up for a deep kiss. Tongue stroking along Ty's, Lewis kissed him stupid and then rutted against Ty's bare cock with his own, fingers pulling them into position and stroking fast. Ty lasted through long minutes of that delicious glide of friction, but when it was heightened by the heat of Lewis' ejaculate coating his cock, it had pulled Ty over the edge before he realized he was so close.

"Dammit." He'd wanted to get Lewis off, and then take things farther. Ty huffed out a laugh, cheek pressed to Lewis' shoulder. "I had all these playtime plans. I wanted to do more for ya."

Lewis' hand coasted up and down his spine, fingertips alternating between a firm stroke and a glancing caress, the effect dragging Ty closer to sleep with every breath. "You do a lot, lover. Let me take care of you."

"You always do." Ty rolled his head, dropping a hard kiss against Lewis' chest.

"Then there's no problem." Lewis' breathing deepened, as if he were on the edge of sleep, but the tension in his muscles put that to a lie.

"I wanna do more. I wanna watch you fall apart." Ty complained, his own voice sleep-roughened. "Wanna do to you what you want. I'm not afraid. Not of you. I trust you. No matter what." Ty realized Lewis had gone completely still. With some effort, he lifted his head

slightly to see that edge of panic back on Lewis' face. "What's wrong?"

Lewis rolled away, easing Ty's head to the pillows. "Gonna go check on Crissy. She's probably asleep at her computer again."

Shoving up on an elbow, Ty swept his hair back with one hand, staring over at Lewis, stomach rolling. "No, something's wrong. What's up?"

Wiping his belly with a pair of boxers, Lewis shook his head, his gaze skittering around the room and landing anywhere except on Ty. "She needs to sleep."

"I'm not disagreeing with you. But that ain't what I'm askin' about and you know it. Tell me what that was just now?" Lewis grabbed a pair of clean underwear from a drawer and pulled them on as he shook his head. Ty was frantic to understand, because whatever he'd done was driving his lover from their bed and into the dark. Lewis— who loved to cuddle even more than Crissy—was abandoning the warmth under the covers and loose muscles that he'd earned, in an effort to avoid something Ty didn't understand. "Lewis, what's wrong? What'd I do?" Lewis slashed a glance his direction, the look so filled with pain Ty's breath clogged in his throat. "Lewis?"

"Just...lemme go check on Crissy." Lewis bent down, molding his lips to Ty's. Firm and strong, the rasp of stubble across his chin left no doubt who Ty was kissing. He licked along Lewis' lips, dueling with his tongue for a moment before Lewis pulled back. Forehead to Ty's,

13

Lewis finally admitted something that made the bile rise in Ty's throat, "We need to talk, but I wanna wait until tomorrow. Okay? Can you give me that?"

Now it was tomorrow, and as much as he loved what Lewis was doing with his mouth, Ty had waited long enough. He used his grip on Lewis' hair to pull him all the way off, staring down at his lover's face.

Eyes half-lidded and dark with desire, Lewis' lips were red, puffy, slick with wet from what he'd been doing. Ty swooped down and captured his mouth, plunged his tongue deep, and licked a long, firm stroke along the inside. Lewis responded in kind, and they dueled for supremacy, Ty retaining the upper hand only barely, angling Lewis' head for a renewed attack, sucking and biting at his lips until the man groaned, the sound making Ty's dick impossibly harder. That sound was what he wanted, that exact noise. *Only more. I want more.* "I love hearing you."

He shifted his grip and tipped Lewis' head to the side, attacking his neck with ferocious hard and sucking kisses, teeth threatening as he worked his way down, and then back up, latching onto Lewis' earlobe with his teeth and eliciting another vibrating groan. "I love making you make those sounds."

Ty brought his other hand up, cupping Lewis' jaw and bringing his chin up. His mouth followed the path of Lewis' Adam's apple, the tang of sweat a deliciously spicy flavor he'd become addicted to. "I love you." Ty pulled back and was staring down into Lewis' face when he said those words so he didn't miss the easing of his features. "You like hearin' that." Lewis nodded against his grip, head moving up and down slightly.

He assessed the location for what he wanted to do. They were both big men, and the chair Lewis sat in was sturdy but not wide. That meant the porch was a no-go, but Crissy was still asleep in their bed, not resting well, not with Lewis staying away all night. None of them slept well away from the others now, having become entirely accustomed to making a three-way puppy pile of tangled legs and arms, hands holding on even in their sleep, heads on shoulders or propped on ribs. It didn't matter how, they were always touching, always in contact, and without that, they just didn't do well.

"I want you." He gave Lewis his desires in a soft statement and saw the instant the walls started to go back up between them. "Don't, man. Don't do that to me." He pressed his mouth to Lewis' neck, letting him feel the edge of teeth with every hard kiss. "Don't make me wonder if you don't like this. Don't make me feel like an intruder, an unwanted distraction. Don't make me feel less than." Lewis bit off a curse, muscles bulging and flexing under Ty's hands as if he were remaining still with only the greatest effort. "Let me in, dammit. I want you, wanna feel you." Frustrated, Ty straightened and urged Lewis to rise to his feet, pressing closer with every movement. "Wanna know I'm still what you want." Lewis' mouth was on the side of his face, lips sliding along his jaw to his ear. "Wanna know you're still in this."

"Oh, baby, be careful what you ask for." Lewis' whisper rasped out slowly, words gaining vowels and sounds as he drawled them out using his deepest backwoods patois. "Be sure you want this."

"I do," Ty reassured him, flattening one hand against Lewis' back, fingers fisting in his shirt to bring their chests together. "God, I do."

"I wanted to talk first." Lewis slipped his palm down Ty's waist, curving around to his ass, gripping firmly, fingers digging in deep to haul their hips into alignment, the rough handling making his breath come quickly. *If he only knew what it does to me*. Lewis reminded him, "I think we needa have a convo, baby."

"Then you shoulda come to bed last night." Ty leaned back only far enough to get his mouth on Lewis', kissing him hard, teeth clashing as their heads angled back and forth, lips working against each other. He used his hold on Lewis' shirt to draw him towards the house and through the door, the kiss never breaking. When his eyes fluttered open, he saw Lewis' were closed, his features twisted in passion. Lewis already looked like he was chasing an orgasm, and Ty wondered if he'd been hungry for this, too. "We can talk later." His guttural mutter was covered on the end by Lewis' husky laughter.

"Okay, baby. We'll talk later. Seems I got some reassurin' to do, and trust me, the things I'm gonna do to you are gonna lay those fears to rest." Lewis' hand slipped up Ty's shoulder, curling around the back of his neck, and a thumb dug under his chin, lifting his mouth for another assault.

Wait.

This wasn't what he'd wanted. This was Lewis taking control again, and Ty knew if he didn't stop things in their tracks now, this encounter would end the way the previous ones had, with Ty pleasured and satisfied...and wondering what had happened to all his plans. If he didn't change directions now, it would be him not getting to do a single thing he'd been dreaming of doing.

Mimicking Lewis' actions from a few moments earlier, he curved an arm around his lover's waist, hand slipping along bare skin as he traced the top edge of the fabric. Locating a gap with touch alone, Ty eased his hand into Lewis' pants, finding him commando as he curled his fingers around the curve of one cheek, springy hair scratchy against his palm. Fingertips wedged into the crease of Lewis' ass, he gripped hard, lifting and pulling in one movement, grinding his rigid shaft against Lewis'. And...Lewis froze.

It was only for the barest of moments, but Ty felt it cut through him. This could all still be tracked back to the night he'd broken up with Lewis and Crissy. *He's wrong.* Ty felt like that mistake would follow him forever. *I'm the one who needs to do the reassuring.* "I want you, Lewis. That means I want to touch you." He adjusted his grip, thrusting with his hips to create more friction. "I wanna feel you." He held Lewis tight with the arm around his shoulders, retrieving his other hand to reach around and cup Lewis' hard cock. "I wanna taste you."

Lewis pulled back and stared at him, gaze dragging down across Ty's features, snagging on his mouth when Ty knowingly licked a long stripe across his lower lip, curling his tongue at the end of the motion. He grinned when Lewis muttered, "Fucker."

Ty lifted his hand and cupped Lewis' cheek, thumb working across that sharp cheekbone, swiping a soft path back and forth under his eye. "That's me." He slow-motion scratched at Lewis' scruff, smiling when the man leaned into the pressure.

"You sure, Tyler? Ain't anything I'll ever demand from you." Lewis shook his head. "Or Crissy, and you know that's a fact." Ty did, having listened to Lewis coach them both on the importance of asking for what they wanted, and speaking up if anything was happening they weren't okay with. "You want things to stay the way they are, we're all good with each other as is. You know? What we have is good. So fucking good. I don't want to fuck it up."

And there it is, Lewis' fear laid bare.

"You didn't fuck it up before, Ralph." If Lewis could pull out his full name, he could do the same. "That's on me. All on me."

"I did. I took before you were ready. I didn't ask what you were going through, just flowed along the surface of everything, and that...Ty, that nearly cost me everything." Lewis swallowed hard, and Ty's gaze tracked the action of that mouthwatering Adam's apple he'd been attentive to earlier. "Nearly cost me everything that matters."

"Actually, you *nearly* saved us weeks of pain." Ty shook his head when Lewis tried to step backwards, following closely. "No, Lewis, you stay right here. I like you up against me, like feeling your strength pitted to mine. You stay right where you are and listen." He narrowed his eyes. "You wanted to talk, I was willing to go without that if we could work it through, but we can't, so we'll talk. But it'll be here on my terms, on our feet, my junk mashed up against yours, the heat of your skin on mine. Because when we're done talking—and by we, I mean *me*, because I'm the one who broke things to begin with—I will still want all the things I want right now." He shrugged, the corner of his mouth lifting crookedly. "Just, maybe you'll believe me then."

"Talk to me. You talk, I'll listen." Lewis grazed his lips across Ty's, the rough bristle of his scruff electrifying. "And then I'll talk." He grinned, the tip of a finger tracing down the curve of Ty's ear. "Then we'll move on to the naked wrasslin'."

"Promise?" Ty heard the question fall from his mouth and he winced, because it sounded so damned hopeful and vulnerable, and way too much like some little thirteen-year-old with a hopeless crush on someone entirely out of his league. *But isn't that the way I feel about 90 percent of the time?*

"Promise you, Tyler." Lewis rested his forehead against Ty's, his eyes slipping closed as he breathed deeply. "I promise you will do everything you've been thinking about. Everything I've been holding off on. Everything."

Chapter Three

Lewis

Knees locked, he stood, chest pressed against Ty's bare one, listening to the man breathe. In and pause, then out in a controlled rush. Lewis deliberately slowed his breathing to match, the heat of Ty's skin radiating through him, hating the coiled tension of the toned muscles under his palm. It took a moment, but Ty finally cleared his throat indicating he was ready to speak. Lewis braced, ready for the worst.

"When you came over that night, I was already worked up for a fight. If you'd've taken a swing at me, it woulda made my damn night, I was that wound up. I'd already smashed Crissy to pieces with my words, left her

21

standin' in her apartment cryin', and I was just holdin' tight to whatever anger I could still muster up, which wasn't a fuck of a lot. It hurt." Lewis opened his eyes when Ty paused, closing them quickly to hide from the pain in his face. "So goddamned bad. Like nothin' I'd ever felt before. You know?"

"I do. I do, Ty. You weren't alone in that."

"No, but I caused it. I made that out of whole cloth, and I knew. I fuckin' knew what I'd done. Lewis, that's the worst thing, the part I can't get past, is I knew in the moment it was the wrong decision, but I couldn't stop it. Not by myself. I couldn't stop it."

"You tried." Lewis offered him an out, not expecting him to take it, and was unsurprised when Ty shook his head, arm tightening around Lewis as he leaned forwards to bury his face in the crook of his neck. *He's carryin' so much fuckin' pain*. It was killing Lewis to hear Ty like this. "Yeah, you fuckin' did, baby. I was there, I know."

"I didn't do enough. I fucked up, and then it was like a slow-motion wreck, you know? I could see it coming and didn't want it, really truly didn't want it, but I couldn't seem to help myself stop it." His shoulders jerked, and Lewis wrapped him up, both arms around his back, holding on tight. "I fuckin' love you, man. I love Crissy, and you, and I still wrecked it all."

"You chased the fuck outta me in that apartment." Lewis stretched the fingers of his hand, reaching for and playing with the ends of Ty's hair that dangled down his back. *We need to get to the fun part of the night, let me put his mind to rest.* "Chased me, pressed me into the wall. Rocked my goddamned world, because it was everything I wanted. That's when my fuckup compounded yours."

"You didn't fuck up." The words burst from Ty as he tried to push away, but this time it was Lewis who held fast. He forced Ty to stay in place until he finally relaxed, head a welcome weight resting on Lewis' shoulder. More than a minute later, Ty picked up the conversation again, the solid embrace seeming to bolster him enough. "You didn't, Lewis. You, everything you did, everything you gave me that day, it scratched and scratched at my anger, wearing down every fear, until—fuckin' finally—there was a moment when everything felt in balance."

"What happened to push it wonky? That's what's been tearin' me up. I don't know what I did to put a stop to it, and it was like you ran into a motherfuckin' brick wall, man. One second you were there, and I knew it was too fast, too much, but you were into it and I...fuck, Tyler. I wanted it so goddamned bad, I let that want overrule my head and what I shoulda done. Then in an instant, you'd slammed on the brakes and we were headed towards that wall. I blinked, and you were shut down, and a moment later I was out the door, closing that on half of the best thing I'd ever held in my hand. I've spent hours tryin' to see where I fucked up. Tryin' to understand how I coulda done different by you, worked things out to keep you. I wanna keep you, Ty. More than anything, I wanna keep you."

"I don't know." The lie colored Ty's voice, made it shake and Lewis shook his head, thinking *I cain't let him get away with that bullshit*. Ty's cheeks colored, but he persisted with more deception. "No, I don't."

"Did I make you feel like that was why I was there? For a blowjob and sex?" Ty's head shook side to side, but he'd fallen mute. *I'm on the trail.* "Like I was only in it for the feel-good times?" Another silent headshake. *Goddammit, give me something.* "Then what, Ty? What happened? You gotta fuckin' talk to me, man. The only way we're gonna get past it is to figure it out. Otherwise, I'm gonna keep fuckin' up, because I'm scared I'm gonna do whatever it was again, make you leave us. Don't leave us, Ty. Don't."

After an extended and frightening silence, Ty offered a not-at-all reassuring, "I won't."

"I'd have said you never would, but what happened, happened, and now it's up to us to sort our shit out so any of us leavin' ain't a worry ever again. You'd talked to Ace earlier that day, right?" Ty sighed, the breath he huffed out sounding angry. "Okay, we'll back up a bit. You said you were down in New Orleans, waitin' on me, but I didn't know, so I didn't show. You spoke to Truman in the bar. What did he say?"

Once more, there was a period of silence that seemed to stretch on for hours. Lewis' heart clenched and ached in his chest, because right now, right here, even holding his lover in his arms, he didn't have full faith that everything would work out. He needed it to, wanted this relationship more than anything, just like he'd told Ty, but without understanding what had enabled the man to walk away before, he didn't have any faith that they wouldn't get there again.

"Boastful asshole." Ty's mutter was low and angry, scarcely more than a whisper, but even that was more than he'd given Lewis in the past few minutes, so he grunted and held his tongue. "He was claimin' you'd fucked him."

The accusation made Lewis' head pound, teeth gritted with fury, but he held tight to his irritation, channeling the emotion into a statement he hoped would draw more out than a question might. "He said more than that."

Added silence, this interrupted by Ty shifting, sliding to the side so he could burrow a little closer all along Lewis' body. *That's good. At least he ain't movin' away.*

Still quiet, Ty's sigh preceded his words by only a breath. "Said you had a cycle, pointed to Greg as an illustration." Lewis' instinctive reaction was to bunch his muscles, preparing for a fight already weeks in the past. He knew Ty had felt the flinch when he whispered softly, "Hush, Lewis. He's dead and gone, and ain't never gonna haunt you again."

"If ever there was someone I regretted fuckin', it'd be that man. And you know I never screwed Truman. I done told you that." He heard the biting edge of anger in his voice and tried to tame it back. "What else was said?

25

You told me all that, but you got caught up in talkin' about Ace hearin' everything, and that's when I got pissed because you were takin' lies and hearsay as truth and fact, and all without asking me. Didn't even ask before you acted. Foolish man, playin' foolish games with the hearts of everyone, because you couldn't be bothered to fuckin' ask a goddamned question." Lewis pulled in a slow breath, unclenched his teeth, and gave a low demand he hoped Ty couldn't ignore. "Now, what else was said that torqued you over?"

"I...I heard the asshole's voice in my head, talkin' about you. I'd been down by the suite, and we were outside Plaisirs Caches. He and I were standin' on the sidewalk and he told me *'Po'Boy doesn't do relationships. It's just sex to him.'* I knew he was wrong, but the idea stuck." Ty's body shook. "He said you played and had your fun, and then when you were done—you were good and *done*. I got spooked about Ace hearin' the call, which he did, but the man clearly doesn't give a shit, because you heard what he's pushin' me for."

Lewis knew Ace was indeed pushing for a change in the CoBos leadership and had made it clear he expected certain commitments from Ty. That played back into the conversation Lewis needed to have with Twisted, but if he allowed Ty this sidebar, they might never get back on track to finally clearing the air. "Bring it back to us for now. We can talk club later, baby." He twisted the strand of Ty's hair around his finger, giving it a tiny tug. "Back to us, yeah?"

"So I got to thinkin' what would happen if you didn't do relationships, if he was right, and realized what the fuck did I know? I didn't have a goddamned clue what I was doin', but I'd never seen you with anyone serious, so it sounded possible. There was a tone to it, the way he said it, like you not doin' a relationship made sense. That meant you'd be scrapin' me off sooner or later, and if Ace had heard me talking about us and was gonna call me to church, if I could say we weren't a thing, weren't in whatever we were in, and it wouldn't be a lie...then maybe I could keep *something*." Broad shoulders heaved under Lewis' touch, and his heart clenched for the pain in Ty's voice. "Keep something, because I knew Crissy was yours. She was yours first, so if there wasn't an us, then there couldn't be a her and me. Why would she pick me when she could have you?"

Fuck. I didn't have any idea. Lewis tipped his head to press against Ty's, embracing him just a little harder, trying to hold him together. *I got you, baby. I'll always have you.*

Ty laughed, the sound broken and tired. "I was afraid, all right? Fucked in the head from what he told me, and I freaked out. Freaked out and fucked up. Scared of losing you, of losing her, of losing the club. So I picked, or I tried to. I picked the club for me, and Crissy for you. I didn't want you to...I don't know. I didn't want to wait for you to drop me, set me aside because you didn't do relationships. Because what if it was just sex to you? What did that leave me? The club." Chest tight, Lewis empathized, because he understood Ty's reasoning far too well. Ty's voice dropped to a rasp, and Lewis felt a renewed stirring against his hip, Ty's cock fattening at whatever was going through his head. A breath later, he understood. "So, when I went down on you, and you were into it...Fuck, you were so goddamned into it, I loved hearing you, seeing you. Knowing I was the one doin' that to you, causin' you to make those noises, I fuckin' loved that. No lies there, brother..." He trailed off slowly, and Lewis waited, rewarded finally by the softly-spoken, "lover." *Yes*. Sweet nothings didn't come easily to Ty, and him using that word in the midst of this painful story spoke volumes to how he felt. *He ain't runnin'*.

Ty didn't pause, the words rushing out of him now. "I loved it. Fuckin' loved it. No lies there. But there was this minute. This single instant of time, when you were coaching me along, and it all sounded so...mechanical. Do this, do that, we'll get off, race to the finish line, and ta-dah." Ty shrugged, his muscles moving under Lewis' hands. "Like something you'd done a thousand times before and would do another thousand after you kicked me to the curb. All I could hear was that motherfuckin' asshole, and he was in my head, man. Stuck like a song you can't get rid of, about to drive you out of your mind. His voice, his words, everything he said, it just...that's what happened. You wanted to know, and now you do. I wasn't givin' you a chance to dump me, because I already was so goddamned deep, it would have killed me. Almost did kill me, being away from the two of you. But I didn't know what else to do."

"A preemptive strike." Lewis muttered the words, lips to Ty's temple. They were swaying gently back and forth, feet stuck in place while he offered the only comfort he could until Ty was done flushing the pain out of his system. "Tell me everything, baby. It's like a poison inside you, baby. Get it all out. Give it to me, I can take it. I can carry it for you. Come on, get it out. What'd you do after I left?"

"Fuck." The cry tore out of Ty, his back bowing sharply. "I just stood for the longest time, stared at a picture of me and Bagger, tried to imagine what he'd tell me to do, but I was so muddled. Then, when I didn't hear your truck, I went and looked out the window." He sucked a slow breath, ribs expanding like a drum. "Saw you was still parked on the lot. Thought that should make it better, seeing it meant you went to our Crissy. You'd told me how tore up she was. Not sleepin', cryin', mourning the death of the thing I'd ripped apart. So I knew you were with Crissy, and that made it better for about a minute. Soothed my soul." His shoulders twitched, as if he were trying to dislodge a burden. Lewis ran a soothing hand up and down the long muscles in his back, stroking and caressing as best he could. "About a minute, then I wondered what you were doing. Would you be with her? Lovin' on her? Would she take to just you again, like y'all had started out with? Was I even missed in that bed you shared? Less than a memory? Fucked with my head, man. I did it to myself, but I knew...I fuckin' knew I'd messed up by the time the door closed behind you. So when it was hours before I saw you walk out of her place and to your truck, and you left without even lookin' my way, it was just done. Everything I wanted was out of reach. I'd seen the best of what I could have, how it could be, and it was gone. And then when Ace didn't bring up what he'd heard, didn't call me to the floor for anything, it hit me."

The silence pressed in on Lewis until he felt like he was suffocating. "You did it for nothing."

"I'd done it for nothing," Ty echoed him. "I fuckin' did all of that for nothing. All the wrong reasons, all the stupid headed ideas, and the thing I thought I was salvaging for myself wasn't even in jeopardy. And I wanted. *God*, I wanted. *Want*. That's a current day thing, lover." The word came easier this time, gently expelled on a sigh. "I can't get enough of you. And I want you to be the same. So, when you dodge my touch, it kills me inside. I need you like I need air. Like I need Crissy."

"Thought we should take it slow gettin' back to where we were."

"Well, you thought wrong, then. It's been slow. Too slow for me."

"And for me," Crissy said, her voice rough with sleep. Lewis looked to the doorway to see her leaned against the frame, hip cocked to the side, dressing gown opened to show the deep garnet of her panties, the silky-smooth skin between her breasts. He'd been so caught up in listening to Ty he'd missed the moment she made an appearance. "You've been all talkie-talkie about everything except this, Lewis. Talkie-talkie about jealousy. Talkie-talkie about not doing things we don't want. Talkie-talkie about not feelin' guilty about takin' what we do want. But here you are, holding onto one of the things you need the most, and you're not followin' your own preachin'." She'd adopted their drawling accent, and when she flashed a bright grin at him, he knew she was trying to lighten the mood. "You want? You take, and we'll give. That's what we want too, anyway. Might as well make all of us happier."

Ty twisted in his arms, and Lewis let him, pulling him back tightly again once he'd turned to face her. "I'm sorry. So fuckin' sorry, Crissy."

The top of her head tipped to one side and she stared at Ty, then nodded slowly. "I know you are. I knew it the night it happened. I knew your regret every time I saw you during those mad, mad weeks. I've already forgiven you, and hearing the real reasons just now, I'm so sorry I held it against you at all. I understand about fear and how that can drive a person to do things they wouldn't normally do. I understand about the way loss can terrify a body into illogical decisions, into bargains with God, and in this case, into driving three people who love each other apart. You're forgiven, Ty. Do you forgive yourself? That's probably the harder question to answer." Lewis renewed his grip around Ty because he could tell her words were hitting him hard, a trembling had set-up in his muscles. *Truth is a bitch, sometimes*. "Because I know you, and you are your own worst critic." She smiled, her features so soft and loving, and that

31

expression was something he liked to see aimed in Ty's direction. *My direction*. As if she heard him, her gaze flicked to his face and she dipped her chin. "But I love you, and I'll keep loving you. Now," she dusted her palms off, fingers ending in a tangle in front of her belly, "can I come over there and hug up on the two of you, or should I go back to bed?"

"Get your ass over here, woman." Ready to hold her close, Lewis raised an arm, shifting Ty to the side slightly. Together they caught her as she threw herself at them, the unsteadiness in her limbs telling him she'd been listening for a while and had been as afraid as Lewis was that this whole scene had been the beginning of Ty breaking up with them again. *Never been so glad to be wrong*. He buried his face in her hair, breathing deeply. "Kiss me, beautiful," he murmured, and she met his questing lips with hers, nearly bringing him to his knees with the trust and love she offered them every day. He kissed her softly, rolling the caress across her supple lips, ending with an affectionate puckered smack he knew she liked. "I fuckin' love you."

"I love fucking you." He laughed and she giggled at her quip, the sound bright and filled with happiness. Then she squealed and jerked sideways, her head lifting to direct a glare at Ty. "No tickles."

"Oh, there will be tickles." Voice deep, husky with renewed desire, Ty brushed the tip of his nose along her cheek. "Unless there are immediate kisses to derail the fingers, there's gonna be a fuckton of tickles. I want to drink my fill, honey."

"Then—" She kissed his nose. "—let me—" She kissed his cheek. "—give you—" She kissed his jaw. "—all the—" She kissed the corner of his mouth, breath catching at whatever Ty's fingers were doing down below. "—all the kisses."

Ty's head dipped and he fused his mouth to hers, muscles in his jaw working as his tongue slipped between her lips. Lewis felt her groaning response rattle through him, settling deep in his belly, cock stiffening and thumping to be released. He'd held onto control for a long time and he relished the idea of loosing that leash.

"Oh, Ty," she whispered when the kiss finally ended, face flushed, mouth open as she panted for air. "You didn't have to carry that alone. Lewis is right."

"Don't tell him that," Ty warned, cutting a teasing glance at Lewis. "He'll get a big head."

"I got your big head," Lewis grumbled, gripping his crotch and giving his dick a stroke through his jeans. "Right here."

"Don't even start, big man," Crissy scolded him. "You're the one who didn't come to bed last night. At least Ty cuddled with me."

"Big man, you got that right." He stroked himself again. "You tellin' me all he did was cuddle? You needin' some love, baby?" Lewis dragged the pad of his thumb firmly up the skin of her belly, offsetting the teasing tickles Ty had plied her with. He twitched the fabric of her gown to the side and cupped a breast in his palm with a rough massage. Her nipple was quick to bud, hardening against his skin, and he plucked at it with his fingers. "Crissy wantin'?" Ty angled his head toward her neck, and Lewis saw a flash of teeth as he nibbled up to her jaw. Her lips parted as she arched her back to stare up at him and Lewis marveled again that everything held in his arms was his for the taking. He wouldn't even have to take; they would both give him everything. *Already do give me all I need.* "Our Crissy feelin' frisky?"

"If I say yes, are you going to follow through, Lewis?" Her eyes flashed and her breath caught just as Lewis' gaze glimpsed Ty's fingers dipping under the gusset of her panties. "God, you guys don't play fair." Eyes closed, she pressed her lips together a moment, then looked at him and asked again, "Will you follow through with asking for what you want?"

"You interested in my needs, baby? Gonna quiz me now or later? You wanna know what turns me on here and now?" Crissy's eyes cut to the side, and he shook his head at her shyness. Bending his neck, he kissed her, taking her mouth suddenly, capturing the tiny sound of surprise she made. His leg pressed between hers, where Ty was moving, the hard edge of his hand pressing against Lewis' thigh in a natural rhythm that came as easy to them as dancing. Lips, teeth, tongue, he used every weapon to tear down her defenses, to bring her down to where honesty would boil over, taking her inhibitions away and leaving the love and emotion bare. "Huh? Wanna know what I like?"

"Mmhmm." Her whisper was breathy and low, and at the sound, his cock gave a gigantic twitch and jerk, leaving what he knew was a wet spot on the front of his jeans and him not giving a shit. If he came in his pants from watching Ty get Crissy off, it wouldn't be the first time and he wouldn't be a lick embarrassed. His lovers were gorgeous together and flowed like water as they loved each other. "Yeah."

"You wanna know everything? Want me to lay it out there?" Ty advanced from the side as Lewis spoke and buried his face against her neck. A second later, Crissy bowed backwards in Lewis' grip. He tightened his arm to hold her upright, taking her weight as her knees grew wobbly. "Wanna know how much I love feelin' my man's hands on me along with my woman's? Wanna know how much it turns me on to feel beard or scruff on my belly, knowing the next moment will be a hot mouth on my cock?"

"Yes," she breathed, and he didn't know if it was in response to him, or what Ty was doing between her legs, and didn't care, because all that mattered was their Crissy feeling their love.

"Yeah, baby. You ridin' his hand like that? Lettin' him finger you while I have your mouth? That's something I like so much. Fuckin' love it. A definite turn on for me." Her hips moved, a subtle back and forth he felt through her body like a wave. "What makes it better is gettin' to

35

watch you get yours, Crissy. See your face when you ride that wave he gives you. Man's got good hands, strong hands, knows his way around a body. Knows how to make it so fuckin' good, don't he? You gonna come, Crissy? Huh? Gonna come on his hand?"

"Please, God, woman." Ty's gruff mutter came like a balm, and Lewis relaxed knowing he was mentally there and present. Listening to Lewis lay himself open like this, it wasn't just Crissy in this with him. The dark tone in Ty's voice told him the man wasn't unaffected, and Lewis liked knowing he could bring that kind of reaction to bear in both his lovers.

"Yeah, come for us, Crissy." He plumped and caressed her breast, thumb and finger reclaiming her tightly-budded nipple, plucking and tugging, rolling in time with her hips. "Come for Ty while he listens to what I want from him. Givin' this to both of you like this, not how I expected, but I'll take what I get. Happy to take everything you'll give me. You wanna know more? Huh? Wanna know more?"

Eyes closed, her head moved in something he interpreted as a nod and he chuckled.

"Awww, yeah. Our Ty, he's a big boy, yeah? That's something else I like. You wanna hear how knowing a man has the strength to hold his own against me is a huge turn on? You already know I like to have my magic button massaged, know how to dig deep in there with your fingers, finding and stroking that while you suck me off. One of the things I'd like to see is Ty taking that from you, laying there and letting you give it to him that way. My mouth on his cock, you fuckin' his ass while he fucks my mouth." He paused for a breath, dick ramrod hard in his jeans, the fabric rough as it shifted over his sensitive head.

"And later? That's when I'd have him in my ass while I'm buried deep inside you, me the go-between, you bucking back against me, riding my cock in your own way while he's plowing me from behind, driving me forwards and backwards with your desires, leaving me to take everything from both of you. That's what I want, Crissy. That's what I want to work up to, and I cannot fuckin' wait to get it."

Faster and faster, the words poured out of him, each one another step along a path he could never unwalk. *I gotta trust 'em. Trust 'em as much as I love 'em.* He knew he had to show how much he believed in them as a triad, a poly relationship could only work with openness. *Show 'em the way.* They'd always looked to him to lead, and this was no different.

"Baby, tell me you want that. Tell me you're okay with it." He'd heard it from Ty's lips but needed to know she wouldn't judge him, still a niggling fear in the back of his mind. "You tell me to take it, I will. If Ty's on board for it, and you are too, then I'm all over every bit of that. I want it, want it all, want to be everything you need, and have you and Ty know that you're it for me. Ain't no worryin' about me runnin' around, about me losin' interest in what's offered—because everything you two are, is *it*. *This*, right here with the two of you, *this* what I've looked for my whole life. I've been lost and looking and wound up here exactly where my heart and soul tells me I'm home. I'm home, Crissy, you and Ty, you're my home and I love you. Love him. Love the both of you."

At some point in his fervent plea, Ty had stopped kissing Crissy and his lovers stared at him, eyes brimming with emotion. He finished, the words scratching his throat raw, because the well of emotion in his chest was overflowing. If felt as if he were negotiating for his life, and in a way, he was. "I just fucking love the two of you."

Crissy gripped his arm tightly and she offered him the brightest smile he'd ever witnessed, full of love and light and pure adoration. Of him. *Of me.* "Oh, Lewis. You never had to worry. There is nothing about you that bears concern I'm going to reject it. You're raw and real, and you own your desires. They're not secrets, and you're not ashamed to say what you need, and I want to give you that. You deserve every good thing, sweetheart. You're our home, too. Mine and Ty's. We belong—" She pursed her lips in a soft air kiss. "—with you." Her eyes slipped closed and she sipped at the air, a quiet moan rattling up from inside her chest. "Ty, please."

"You gonna come, Crissy?" Ty kept his eyes on Lewis as he spoke, and Lewis felt them like a weight. He was poised motionless, not sure what Ty was asking for. Then Ty showed he wasn't always gonna follow, that he wanted to lead sometimes, as he'd tried over the past weeks even as Lewis had tried to shut him down. With a chin lift, Ty demanded, "Come here."

His lips remained parted after the final syllable, and Lewis gave Ty his mouth, letting his lover own him that way, while he was owning Crissy's reactions in others. Soft and hard by unequal measures, Ty's velvet tongue stroked while his lips pressed firmly, unshaven scruff sending shoots of electricity down Lewis' spine with each movement. Crissy's head rested on his shoulder and her fingers dug deeply, body jolting with signals he and Ty knew well. *She's so fuckin' close*. Ty's arm shifted against Lewis' side, lips moving across his mouth, Crissy's undulating body stirring in his arms, and it was perfect.

With a groan, he unfastened his pants, yanking the buttons free in a rush. He shoved them down slightly, enough to free himself, then began roughly stripping his cock in time with the movement of Ty's hand pleasuring Crissy. He broke the kiss and pulled back to stare into Ty's eyes. "Want you to come, lover. Want you to come with me, Ty. I got our Crissy. I'll hold her up. You get your dick out and race me. Race me, baby. I won't let her fall. I won't let you down. Promise, baby. Fuckin' promise you the world, if you give me you like this."

Crissy somehow intuited what he wanted, and she reached up and spread her gown wider, showing off her breasts in a way that made him impossibly harder. "Fuck, yeah, Crissy girl. Own that gorgeous body. Goddamn love when you show us that, show us you, put it all out there for both of us."

His dick was leaking constantly now, the slick liquid easing the way of his hand, taking the edge of pain away and leaving only pleasure. He glanced down and saw Ty's cock in his hand, fist pumping fast.

"Lewis." Broken and wrecked, Ty's voice rolled across Lewis like a physical touch. "Wanna see you come."

"Make Crissy come first." Lewis was firmly back in commanding mode, but that was okay. This was familiar and comfortable for all of them, and the group needed a leader. He and Ty could trade off, Crissy could take the main role—it didn't matter, as long as they all got off and felt loved. "Make her know how much we love her, show her."

He kept his eyes on them both, seeing Crissy's head sag backwards as she gasped, hand reaching up to grip the back of Ty's neck, helping hold herself upright, Lewis' arm still firm at her back. "I'm close, sweets," she whispered, then her hips jerked again, and again and her cry rose to the ceiling. Ty's grunts of effort didn't slow, his hand keeping pace with her passion, pulling every quiver and groan from her as Lewis imagined how she'd tightened around his fingers, her inner walls pulsing like his cock would in just a fast minute.

"Gonna come, Ty," he gritted between clenched teeth. "Seein' our Crissy like that does it for me." Balls drawn up tight to his body, he groaned as the fierce tingle circled high up his spine, working from between his cheeks. Ass clenched rock hard, he held his breath and then was coming, brightness lighting up the insides of his eyelids at the first hard rush of semen streamed out of his cock. He slitted his eyes open, watching Crissy's face as he came on her belly and breasts a second time, laying another string of white across her body. A third pulse, not as hard, covered her belly and Ty's wrist. He caught the rest in his hand, making a smeary mess on his cock, pushing through the heat and wet that was a poor imitation of what Crissy could offer, but seeing her covered in him was worth everything.

Then it got better. So much better.

Ty lurched against Lewis, his hand rose from between Crissy's legs to her waist and drew her towards him as he came, the first arc of ejaculate landing between her breasts, the next mixing with Lewis' on her belly. "God." Ty's head dropped, chin to his neck as he watched himself paint her over and over, thumb digging deep into her skin as he held tight. Lewis pulled her closer, his arm across her back holding steady.

Knees weak, Lewis looked at them and chuckled, laughing louder when Crissy's eyes shifted to him. She was smiling, too. Ty looked wrung out, exhausted. Lewis released his cock, wrapping that arm around Ty's back, hand fisted to keep Ty's shirt clean. "We made a mess." Ty grunted and Crissy laughed.

Then she turned the tables on him in a way he couldn't have anticipated, fingers trailing in the spunk sprayed across her torso, mixing his and Ty's streams until there was no more Lewis' and his, just a mess of theirs. She brought a finger to her lips, tongue curling around and licking until it was clear and clean. He groaned and opened his mouth, waiting patiently until Crissy relented and scooped up another fingerful to feed to him. He saw Ty move and wasn't surprised when the next finger at his mouth was male, larger, rough and calloused. Then Crissy's finger, followed by Ty's, and he realized his lovers were giving him the one unspoken thing he also wanted, needed, loved even more because it was them. All of them.

He made sure Crissy was steady on her feet, released Ty to stand on his own, then Lewis dropped to his haunches in the living room and paid homage to his lovers, tongue working across skin and hair, lapping and sucking. Moving from place to place, he had a tit in his mouth one moment, then Ty's softening cock, Crissy's belly quivering under his ministrations, Ty's fingers covered in her salt and musk, Crissy's pussy still wet and hot and sensitive. Lewis worked in silence until Ty hit his knees beside him.

Stunned at the thought, Lewis rested a knee on the floor as he turned to look, and Ty caught him in a deep kiss, tongues working slowly together. Then Ty joined him in tending to Crissy, their mouths moving across her skin. Crissy gripped his hand and lifted it to her lips, her intention clear, and Lewis unclenched his fist, giving her access to perform the same service for him.

This is how we set things right, he thought, mind still reeling with the idea of Ty sharing this with him. *By building a bond over what we want and then showing how we love each other in every way*. "I'm ready for bed," he announced, eyes closing in pleasure when they both laughed at him. That happy sound was worth everything. "This, all of this?" He stood and bent Crissy across his arm, kissing her softly. "Exactly everything I want." She clutched at his shoulders and ate his gasp of surprise down when Ty's mouth covered his cock, pulling it into his mouth and rolling it across his tongue, doing the final bit of housekeeping from their interlude. "Jesus, Ty."

The sensation was overwhelming, heat and suction, then tongue and the barest hint of teeth. A firm, large hand on his thigh slipped up to grip his shaft, angling it so Ty could cover every inch. He worked methodically, ensuring all traces of Lewis' orgasm were wiped clean.

"You want that, Ty?" Head bobbing, Ty made a garbled sound, then hummed. "Fuck, baby. Gonna make me hard again." At his words, Ty redoubled his efforts, and Crissy laughed softly, her head resting on Lewis' chest, chin angled down to watch their lover. "I really need to lay down, Ty. You gonna be pissed I call for a rain check?"

Ty pulled off with a pop and a slurp, and Lewis stared down in awe as the tip of his cock brushed Ty's cheek, connecting a second time when he shook his head slightly. "No, not mad. But I'm gonna hold you to that." He opened his mouth and curled his tongue around the crown, hand holding Lewis' dick in place for a moment as he sucked. "I totally get why you like to play when we're soft, Crissy. I understand now. The possibility is so rich, right there, and you can feel it, like you know what'll happen eventually, but there's something about it in my mouth." He chuckled as he brought the head back to his mouth and slurped on it like a lollipop.

God, this man. "Enough," Lewis said through his laughter as he pulled his hips back. "Enough. Too sensitive."

"Let's go to bed," Crissy said, taking a step backwards. "Come on, Ty. Last one there gets to sleep in the middle." That was enough to get Ty up and moving, and Lewis watched as the pair raced each other to the bedroom, Ty curling an arm around her waist at the last second and pulling her close for a deep kiss before he lifted and threw her, laughing, onto the mattress.

That caress had nothing to do with him, and he was surprised at how much that knowledge settled him. No jealousy in his heart at all. He loved knowing they carried strong feelings for each other. That was how it should be. They had to all be invested with the individuals to make this work, and if anything happened to change the dynamics, their joined lives could shred apart so easily.

Chapter Four
Ty

He lay sandwiched between his lovers, Lewis having argued for the outside spot. Buried face first in the pillow, Lewis' head was level with his, chin scarcely turned to the side to create space for breathing. No matter, he was asleep. His hand and arm were draped possessively across Ty's waist and hip. Crissy pressed tightly to his other side, cheek cradled on his shoulder, her lips bowing and moving with each sleeping breath.

There hadn't been much chatter as they retreated to the bed, Lewis' weariness from his sleepless night apparent, and Crissy's yawns laughable as she professed she wasn't as worn out as she seemed after enjoying such a hard orgasm.

They'd all climaxed, which was a good goal when they fooled around together. But, it wasn't about keeping a tally sheet or being competitive, but more the mutual love and caring they had for each other. Ty wanted to see them pleasured and sated, and knew they felt the same way.

Lewis had surprised him tonight more than once and in all the best ways. First when he'd listened and heard the aching between the words, knew where Ty was coming from with his fears, and effortlessly pulled the painful confession out of him. It had been like a dam breaking, the release of pressure enormous, a relief he hadn't expected.

That was all Lewis, too. Ty sighed. Anyone who knew only the biker side of the man was missing out on so much. This man, the person who'd held him as he wept. The sensitive lover who reminded him that he hadn't lost their love, that through everything, he'd still managed to hold onto them both, against all odds; each facet was one simple aspect of his personality. The whole was so much more, and Ty knew he could dig for days and never get to the end of good surprises. He suspected Twisted was the only one who knew Lewis like that, outside of Ty and Crissy.

Still, Lewis had exposed more than he thought. Ty would be digging into the reaction he'd seen surrounding Greg's betrayal of Lewis soon. Not today, though. Today would be nothing more than a cuddle fest between the three of them. He was determined that right now, at this moment, the outside world would be held at bay, leaving them free to explore the new depths of their shared relationship.

Ty had been stunned for a moment when at the end, after weeks of seeming indecision, Lewis hadn't balked to take everything offered, trusting and believing his partners through it all. Overcome by curiosity, holding to the best part of the memories of sucking Lewis before, Ty had joined in. The taste had at first been overwhelming, foreign and yet familiar from experiencing it in after-kisses. But seeing the excitement on Lewis' face, he couldn't help but get caught up in everything.

And when Lewis had risen to his feet to care for Crissy, bringing her into the shared experience with a kiss that was sensual and hot to watch, Ty couldn't wait. Didn't want to, and applied himself to dealing with that desire immediately. The texture and sensation of Lewis' soft cock had been so starkly different, he'd found himself trying to catalog it, finally giving up and just enjoying the sensations of Lewis' thighs under his hands, tense muscles contracting, Crissy's fingers in his hair stroking through over and over, and the smell and taste of Lewis. Nothing mixed in, nothing to distract, nothing to dilute the essence, and in that moment, Ty was certain he'd found an addiction he didn't mind having.

So, next steps? Blinking against the sun filtering in around the curtains, Ty ran every moment of this morning back through his head. And again. He didn't want to lose this Lewis, didn't want to give the man a chance to retreat to the careful distances and controlled encounters. He much preferred wild Lewis, the man he'd first shared a bed with Crissy with, the one who'd blown his load all over their woman tonight, urging Ty to do the same. It mattered to the long-term viability of them as a threesome, because Crissy was strong-willed, but all of them knew Lewis was their undisputed founder. The man liked to say Crissy was the glue that held them together, but Ty was convinced it was Lewis. He'd created a connection with Crissy first, then opened it up to include Ty, as an equal, not secondary.

A unique and difficult balance to control and maintain, but they'd managed it for what seemed like a long time. Like balancing rocks, the trick was in finding where the unevenness existed and leveraging those rough edges to best advantage, accepting them as given and moving on. *A cairn of love*. He snickered at his thoughts. But still, through weeks turning into months, it had been easy as breathing. *Until I fucked it up*. He shushed his inner critic, preferring instead to focus on what Crissy had said, what Lewis had told him today. Forgiven. Redeemed.

So, if Lewis is the leader, how do I steer things to where I want?

Crissy wasn't above using one of them to influence the other when she wanted something specific from both. Just last week she'd curled up beside Ty on the couch during a movie and whispered dirty nothings in his ear until he scooped her up and carried her to bed. Sitting astride him, she'd already been impaled on his cock before she whispered to Ty about wanting a shared scene like they'd done before. He hadn't hesitated, calling out to Lewis to join them.

Lewis paused in the doorway, arms folded across his chest as he stared at them on the bed. A slow smile split his lips, spreading them until his tongue dipped out, lapping at the air. Crissy lifted slowly and held at the apex of the movement, the head of Ty's cock all that remained inside her. "You invitin' me to the party, Crissy mine?" Ty gripped her hips and pushed up, fucking her from underneath until the slapping of flesh on flesh filled the room. "Looks like you're all full up, honey."

"Get your ass over here." Ty blinked sweat out of his eyes, focused on the sounds Crissy made as she moved on top of him. "She ain't talkin' right now, being as I'm—" He powered up into her a half a dozen times, then slowed the pace, wanting to make it last now that he knew what her intention was. "—fuckin' her up so she can't speak."

"I can," she gasped, and her fingers dug into his chest as he rolled his hips, driving deep. After a moment, she continued, breathless, with tiny pauses between each word that said he was hitting all the right spots. "Speak for myself, thank you." One arm stretched towards the door, the other covered her mouth. Ty saw her bite down on her fingers for a moment, her skin going bloodless and

white beneath the grip of her teeth. "Please," she finally got out. "Please, Lewis."

"Lose the pants," Ty ordered, and Lewis grinned that secretive smile, the one he kept just for them, the one that had driven Ty to chase him for a taste of the forbidden.

"Happy to, baby. A man can't say no to a woman who begs sweet as that, and a man who moves like you do. Work that cock, baby." Lewis thumbed the fastening on his jeans free, making quick work out of removing them. "You don't gotta ask me twice."

"Not that I was askin'." Ty thrust his head back into the pillow, eyes on Crissy as she whined. She still had a hand outstretched to Lewis, but the other was splayed across Ty's chest, holding herself upright. "You close, Crissy? You close, huh?" He sped up again and kept his gaze flicking from her face to the pulse in her throat where it beat hard against the skin, drumming out the pace of her pleasure. Pupils blown wide and dark, she stared down at him and nodded, then her head dropped forwards and she tensed, her core tightening around him. He slowed immediately, and she keened. "No, no. You gotta hold off, baby. Don't come. Wait for Lewis."

They'd learned that if she came first, it was harder for her to ride the wave with the two of them. She did well edging, and Ty worked that angle with her now.

"Don't come, baby." She tightened around him again, muscles in her legs growing taut and her fingers turning to claws, knuckles lifting momentarily. He slowed *his thrusts and dropped his hips, waiting until she chased his cock down to bring his hands to her back. "Lay on me, Crissy. You want Lewis with us?" She nodded, easing forwards, and he crooned into her ear, "Lay on me. Let me hold you. I can hold you, sweetheart." He slowed more, and more, until the movement was more a gentle rocking than the thrusting from before.*

"You got me now, boyo." Lewis' voice came from over Crissy, and Ty clenched in anticipation of the first touch, more ready than he could explain. "Our Crissy's needy, and we have exactly the fix for this hunger of hers."

Lewis' palm trailed a hot path from the inside of Ty's leg to his groin, and Crissy gasped at the same time, clearly experiencing a similar touch. Ty's teeth gritted together, and he swallowed a groan of pleasure when Lewis' finger and thumb circled the base of his cock, firmly jacking up and down the exposed couple of inches. Crissy's muscles flexed under his hand and her channel clenched around the head of his cock. Lewis chuckled darkly when Ty's balls swiftly drew up.

"Ah, God."

Hot breath hit his sac as Lewis' grip tightened to the point of aching, then that was forgotten when heat lapped at his balls, one testicle then the other sucked into the inferno of Lewis' mouth. Crissy's teeth worried at Ty's shoulder, his neck, her fingernails flicking his nipples as she tightened her pussy rhythmically. Ty felt matching jolts all through her body and realized Lewis was setting the pace, slapping her ass in soft tempo. Lewis abandoned his balls, tongue gliding down a moment and Ty lifted his ass, heels digging deep into the soft mattress that had been Lewis' first purchase for the house he'd bought them. His thoughts skittered around that knowledge, because the change in circumstances wasn't yet comfortable, and Ty wanted to stay immersed in the moment.

"Sweet Jesus."

He was overwhelmed in an instant. Sucked under the river of sensation that was his entire focus. Lewis' tongue was on his hole, circling and flicking, the ring of his grip jacking Ty's shaft, and Crissy writhing on his cock as something pressed inside him. "Yes, yes, yes." It was hot and slippery, and Ty realized Lewis was rimming him and thrusting deep at the same time, then rimming again. Finger and tongue, maybe? What the fuck's it matter? Feels goddamned good either way.

None of this was anything they'd done before, but the way it jolted electricity up his backbone in waves, crashing against his brain, it was something he was entirely on board with happening now. And again. And probably again. The sensation peaked and peaked, then ebbed only to lift higher again until Ty was panting out Lewis' name, cursing with every other breath because he'd screwed up their time together. Coulda had this all along.

Lewis' tongue worked deeper for a moment, and Ty's orgasm swelled again, impossibly huge, a giant stomping through his belly. Then it was gone in a flash when Lewis turned his face, rough beard rasping the insides of Ty's cheeks before he retreated, a sense of loss even while he was licking and nibbling his way up to where Ty's cock was still buried in Crissy.

She whined again, the sound coming from far back in her throat. "Be still, sweet girl. Be still on our Ty. He's on edge now, honey. Don't make him come." Lewis' instructions drifted through the air and Crissy nodded, her hair falling around Ty's face as she locked into place. "All of us gonna find ours tonight. Ain't no rush for it, right?"

"Speak for yourself," Ty managed to mumble, stars still shooting behind his lids. "I feel like I already popped one, but I'm still ready to go."

"Magic fuckin' button, baby. Magic fuckin' button." Lewis chuckled, and Ty could only imagine the smile on his face. "When you know, you know."

"Fucking hell. Do it again." Crissy laughed at his demand, then gasped, and the muscles in her pussy rippled, pulling his cock deeper. "Or that, whatever you just did, do that again to our girl. Aww, yeah, that's fine."

She panted hard, then keened, her body shaking. "I'm gonna come, Lewis."

"No, baby. Hold it back. Lemme just get you ready for me." Pressure against the head of Ty's cock meant Lewis had at least one finger in her ass, easing her open for his dick. "Mmmm. God, you are always so fucking tight. So good, Crissy. You're perfect for us, ain't she, Ty?"

"Yes, God, yes. There's just the two of you for me, no one else. Both," something touched his ass again and he broke off, sucking in a hard breath as Lewis' wet, slippery finger pressed and pressed, then broke through the outer ring, dragging in and out slowly. "Guh." He twisted his head so he could bury his face against Crissy. Lightning shattered his spine again as heat filled his belly. His cock swelled, blood pounding through the shaft, and he held still, afraid he'd break the spell if he moved. "Ah, fuck. Fuck, man. Fuck."

"I'm thinkin' we found somethin' our Ty likes, Crissy girl." Lewis groaned. "He's just as tight as you are, baby." The sensation backed off, fading as Lewis withdrew his finger, and Ty arched his back, the renewed deep sense of loss making him rock his hips. "Ah, yeah, chase me, Ty. Chase me and you'll catch me. Just not right this minute. I ain't runnin' far, but I have a date with our Crissy's sweet, sweet ass. Now, that's not to say your ass ain't sweet, because trust me, it fuckin' is. But our Crissy—" Pressure against his dick increased, and Lewis' fingers stroked along his base from inside her. "—comes first."

"She ready?" Ty tightened his abs, cock jerking hard, making Crissy gasp when he did it again, and again. He was on edge emotionally, riding the boundaries of being angry, but for no reason he could understand. It didn't matter the why right now the reaction was threatening to overwhelm him. What the fuck's wrong with me? He knew if he weren't in the position where he was both under and inside Crissy right now, he'd be beating a quick retreat until he could figure out what had just happened.

"Get the lead out, asshole. We gonna do this today sometime?"

Lewis' face appeared from behind Crissy, a frown tucking his brows together. He studied Ty for a moment, then dipped closer, chin hooking over the point of her shoulder.

"Kiss me, lover mine," Lewis demanded. "I can't manage to stroke you like that while I'm in her, but I promise that someday soon, I'll blow your mind with some backdoor bliss like you ain't never imagined. Now, Tyler, kiss me." He did, aggressively lifting his face to meet Lewis', tongues tangling without hesitation. He let Lewis thrust into his mouth and then fit his lips and teeth over the invading tongue that filled him, sucking hard for a moment before going back to a supple twisting and stroking. A minute passed, and another, and Ty dropped into an easier rhythm, letting Lewis take the lead, following closely. Crissy made an approving hum from beside Ty's head as Lewis pulled back. "You better, Ty?" Ty nodded, the unfounded anger having vanished. "Edging is hard on the mind, sometimes. Yours clear now?" Ty nodded again. "Alrighty then. Here we go."

Crissy swooped in and kissed Lewis, neck twisted to reach his mouth and he gave her the same attentive effort he'd given Ty a moment before. Ty watched as their mouths moved, tongues dipping in and out of view, the lush, wet noises playing with his mind until they nearly sounded like fucking.

He imagined Lewis fucking her, but the movie playing out in his head became confused, because for a split second it was him Lewis was fucking, Ty's dick sheathed in Crissy's pussy. He clenched the muscles low in his belly, moving inside her shallowly, waiting. The instant Lewis broke the kiss, Ty was in there, taking ownership of her mouth, tasting Lewis and Crissy mixed, their flavors blended in a way he loved. She stilled on top of him and stiffened, then relaxed, the kiss slowing as he felt the blunt head of Lewis' cock entering her.

"So much," she whimpered, and Lewis shushed her quietly, the pressure lessening for a moment before he moved again, pushing deeper. "Please, more. Love me, Lewis." It went like that for minutes, Ty holding still unless directed otherwise, Lewis advancing and retreating as Crissy grew accustomed to taking them both.

They hit a rhythm finally, a pattern of push and pull, and Ty loved feeling how Crissy moved with each of them differently. His cock had remained stiff and hard, head mushroomed out broad, seminal fluid mixing with what Crissy effortlessly gave him to create a slip and slide for his in-and-out movements. Lewis kept up his coaching through most of it, his voice dipping into a guttural gasp when Crissy arched her back. "Fuck, baby. Do that again." Her torso rolled, shoulders lifting and ass raising, then the small of her back arcing up in a bow. "Jesus, Crissy. Work that ass, baby. How I love fuckin' you with Ty, our Ty and I feel how he's moving. He's in and I'm out, and then I'm in deep again. Clamp down around me, I'm still pullin' out and back in, givin' this to you. Take what you need, baby, take it." Ty reached up a hand and Lewis pressed his mouth to it, lips and teeth against his palm. Ty curved his fingers around the back of Lewis' neck, thumb to his carotid, pulse pounding under his touch. "Aw, yeah, take what you want, Ty baby. Take what you want."

But then Lewis reared back and out of reach, and Ty felt the sting of disappointment. That didn't last long, because a moment later, Lewis' hands were cupping Crissy's shoulders, pulling her back into him, shifting her back and forth on both their cocks.

"Jesus, that's so good." Ty normally wasn't too vocal during sex, but tonight felt different. Lewis was urging them both to do what felt right and talking to his lovers, his partners, the people who mattered most in his world—that felt right. "Crissy's gorgeous, isn't she, Lewis?" Every word came out separate, a burst of sound bracketed by a panting breath. "She loves us. You can see it in her face. Flushed, lips rosy, but the smile she's wearin' is the only thing I wanna see on her. She loves us, and we love her. And this is always—" Crissy moved just right, and he shouted, the sound echoing through the room, "God, baby. This is fuckin' perfect. This, us." He stared at Lewis, watching his face change as emotion rolled over him. Emotion and passion, because he picked up the pace, showing he was just as susceptible to what she did to them as Ty was. "You, Lewis. You're so goddamned perfect for us. For me."

Lewis' head tipped back, a cry bursting from his lips as his body locked up, dick shoved deep as he came. Ty

57

could feel the pulses of heat radiating from Lewis' cock. Crissy was mewling softly, head shaking back and forth, hair trailing across Ty's chest. He shoved a hand between them and lined up a finger on either side of her clit, knowing she needed more to get off right now, because it had been so good. Too good, if such a thing existed, and she needed a big push to get her over the hump and on the downward slide. He angled his heels out and lifted his hips, letting the push of his pelvis grind his fingers into her sex. She drew air through her nose, hard, letting it out on a high whine, and he stroked either side of her clit. Then when she groaned, he pinched, feeling the blood pulsing under his fingers.

Something brushed his chest, the back of Lewis' hand as he reached around to cup Crissy's breast. Ty kept the pace, plunging deep, his cock sliding alongside Lewis' still-hard dick inside her and the friction was incredible. Soft, slick, hard, wet—everything he wanted right here.

"Come for us, Crissy. Come, baby girl, now's your time, baby. Come." Lewis had leaned over her back, mouth to the side of her head and Ty saw her lobe clasped between his teeth. "No more waitin', Crissy. Come, honey."

She stiffened and her back rolled, hips crashing against Ty's as she tightened around him a final time, her pussy pulling him deeper and then Lewis' hand was in front of Ty's face, thumb grazing across his lips and Ty pulled it inside, sucking hard, coming along with Crissy as she broke apart between them, connected to Lewis by *her. Words were lost in sensation as he was flung higher than ever before, the climax seeming to spin on forever, lights and sounds and everything subsumed by the feeling of being here, with them, with her and him, and they were his.* Mine. *That was his last thought before he fell deep and hard, tension flowing away and relaxing finally, Crissy still tightening rhythmically around him. Then Lewis' mouth was on his cock as he freed it from Crissy's sheath, the hot suction pulling a couple of final pulses from him. Crissy hummed contentedly, and Ty knew Lewis was taking care of her, too.*

No, their Crissy hadn't been shy about what she'd wanted. *I just gotta find the same confidence.* He rolled his eyes and sighed. Easier thought than done. *Maybe I need to do research, so I'll know what I'm doing?* His brain flicked back to the memory of him on his knees weeks ago, and again tonight, where there'd been no fumbling either time. So, that act came easy enough to him. He moved restlessly, and Lewis' fingers tightened on his hip, holding him in place. The promised backdoor bliss hadn't happened, even when Ty had suggestively placed Lewis' hand on his ass once. *Once, like that makes me a confident prick.* He squeezed his eyes closed against the light.

In bed with these two was the only place he felt adrift. The rest of his life was metered, measured, and controlled. He knew what his role was and how to fill it, even when it changed, shifted, it was something he'd seen modeled enough that it felt comfortable to pull it on like a cloak. He gave a mental shrug. Maybe research wasn't that bad an idea.

Chapter Five
Lewis

"You know I don't give a shit about that." Twisted angled his neck to look over his shoulder back at Po'Boy.

Here he was fully the MC officer persona, and other than occasional flashes of humor, Lewis slumbered in the back of his mind.

They were standing in the office of the Mandeville clubhouse, watching out the window as Wildman and five or six other members worked their way around the various stations of the homemade gym set up in the back lot. Wildman was currently working on his long-time least favorite activity, inclined sit-ups. With every full extension up, he lifted his hand and flung a bird at the window as he shouted something Po'Boy expected was a strained "fuck you," his normal conversation level when working out.

"I know you don't, and neither do ninety-five out of a hundred members. CoBos are smaller, boss. It matters more that he have their support." Po'Boy shrugged. "Ace steppin' down is a big deal, and Wrench is the only heir apparent. He needs me, brother."

"I need you." Twisted turned from the window and faced him, fisted hands resting on the top of the desk.

"Ain't the same and you know it." Po'Boy stepped backwards and sat on the arm of the couch. "I'm tryin' to make shit work here, man. It's hard as fuck, and I'm not convinced I'm doin' even a half-assed job. I love the club, you know I do. Me bein' your ride or die won't change one whit. You cain't get rid of me, not even if you tried hard. But it's going to come to a decision, and soon, and I don't want you to be...fuck, Twisted. I don't want to lose you. I keep you, keep the boys, then it's like I keep the club."

"Penny likes him for you." Po'Boy rolled his eyes and Twisted laughed. "No, man. She does. She's been different lately, and I ain't sure what's goin' on, but the one thing she's solid on is liking you and Wrench, and that Crissy gal together. Makes her weepy-eyed."

Po'Boy didn't try to suppress his grin. "Ain't me makin' her weepy-eyed, brother. That's a side effect of that bun she's got cookin'. She still feelin' well otherwise?"

His heart warmed at the look that came over Twisted. The softening of his expression was wonderful to see, and the love for his woman shone from inside him. He wondered what it would feel like to know the woman he loved was carrying his child. *Or Wrench's kiddo*. He shook himself, and Twisted studied him for a moment, expression puzzled.

"Yeah, she's past the sick-up phase pretty much. Now she's at the eat-everything-in-the-house phase, which makes her a bit testy in other ways. She's gained like eight pounds." He rolled his eyes. "Looks good on her, but she's worried. I've found there's no way a man can tell a woman he likes her ass that's going to make it okay in her mind."

"How you fixin' that, brother? You needa keep Yousa happy, or I'll be climbin' up *your* ass about it." Po'Boy tossed him a glower he couldn't hold, laughing halfway through.

"I keep tellin' her and showin' her. All a man can do." Twisted leaned back, shoulders on the wall as he folded his arms across his chest. "You and your crew gonna help populate the bayous? Your woman'd make pretty babies, no matter the seed that spawned them."

Po'Boy huffed a laugh. "We're still new. It's early yet to be talkin' a crop of kids." He paused. "You think she wants kids?"

"Shouldn't that be a thing you know, brother?" Twisted chuckled. "Mebbe you should ask your man, too?"

"Fuck you." Said without heat, his words brought another grin to Twisted's face, beard splitting to show a flash of white teeth. A year ago, that would have made Po'Boy crazy, sent him across the causeway to New Orleans and his suite, where he'd bury himself in flesh and forgetfulness. *Now I don't wanna forget a single minute with my two*. It was a good difference, and only possible because of Twisted's acceptance of every part of Po'Boy. Something he'd never expected. "Love you, brother."

"Ditto."

A pounding on the window made them both look, and Po'Boy burst into laughter at the image of Wildman standing right in front, posing, muscles on display. The man turned and tugged his jeans down, showing half an ass cheek as he looked over his shoulder, a provocative smile pursing his lips.

"Don't make promises you ain't ready to back up, brother," Po'Boy called out, shaking his head when Wildman pretended to look shocked, yanking his jeans up high, backing away from the window with both hands spread across his ass. "Fuck you."

"Fuck you, too," Wildman called back cheerfully, laughing as he turned around. That stopped immediately, and he flung his hands towards the sky. "The fuck you think you're lookin' at?" He shouted at the two prospects who'd stopped to watch the exchange. "Get your goddamned probie asses back into it. Fucking hell, you don't stop until I tell you to stop, and then you thank me for letting you goddamned breathe."

"He was a good pick up." Twisted knocked on the window, and Wildman turned around, hand cocked behind his ear indicating he was listening. "Kick ass, Wild. Make 'em work for it. They gotta want it."

With a nod, Wildman shouted back, "Quack, quack," and both Twisted and Po'Boy roared with laughter at the inside joke now shared with another member.

"Lotta things I'll miss, you know? He's one of 'em." Wildman had been Po'Boy's prospect, and in the time since he'd joined the club, he'd come a long way towards trusting the members. "You should take him to Retro's next time you go, give him a broader understanding of how the world works."

Retro was president of a club in Alabama. While small, the friendly club had a long reach, Retro having cultivated connections all over the world. He was the go-to guy when anyone in the south needed info, and both Po'Boy and Twisted counted him a personal friend, in addition to a brother.

"I'll do that." Twisted turned and stared at him for a long minute. "There ain't really no other way, is there?"

Po'Boy shook his head.

"Well, fuck."

Chapter Six

Ty

"Fuck."

It was days after their connection in the living room, and he was finally home alone. He'd planned to do this sooner, but club business needed to be handled. Ace was stepping down as president of the CoBos at the next officer vote and, as he'd threatened to do in the past, had already thrown Wrench's name in the mix as his replacement. There'd been only a few grumbles from members, and Wrench knew he could chalk most of those up to the fact they just didn't like change, not anything aimed at him in particular.

With one member, however, it was a different story.

Aptly named Alcatraz, the old-school biker had spent more time than any other member in Louisiana's Federal Penitentiary called The Farm, and Angola hadn't been kind to him. He hadn't gone inside on account of club business, but the CoBos never turned their backs on a member who was in jail, so his commissary chits and prison account had been kept up to date, and when the bank threatened to take his house, they'd bought the building, giving his old lady a place to shelter until her old man got out.

The first time.

Alcatraz hadn't learned, and within a year of his release, he'd been back inside, this for a longer stint. Wrench had been barely fifteen at the time but raised around the club as he'd been, he'd heard more than one whispered conversation never meant for his ears.

So now, when Alcatraz wanted to talk shit about him and Po'Boy, Wrench had resolved to not let it go. Three days ago, Ace had made his general announcement during a mandatory, all-member meeting and stated his case for Wrench to take up the gavel. Alcatraz had walked out, spewing bullshit along the way about faggots and the club going to the dogs. The man had come back to the clubhouse early the next morning, looking like something the cat dragged in, and drunk enough he'd dropped his bike in the lot and left it laying on its side.

That kind of behavior couldn't go uncontested, because all it took was one soured member to fuck up an entire club. They'd seen it happen to various organizations across Louisiana through the years, and Wrench was damned if he would let it happen to the club his old man had been so proud to be part of.

So yesterday, even if it'd been the last thing he'd wanted to do, Wrench lay in wait for the man to wake. He'd had a prospect care for the bike, picking it up and parking it properly, but then had pocketed the keys, which meant Alcatraz couldn't avoid him if he didn't want to have to hotwire his own ride.

That conversation had gone about as well as Wrench had expected. He'd sat and listened to the blustering fool going on about protocol and rules, waiting until the old man had run out of steam. However, once he'd calmed enough to sit across a table from Wrench, he'd clammed up, refusing to engage for more than single word responses.

After handing over the man's keys, Wrench had watched him stalk out of the clubhouse, frowning at the carefully closed door. He'd almost have rather a slam, because that'd mean heated emotions were in charge. A closed door carried a different distinction, and Wrench had texted Ace with, **Not sure he's salvageable**, receiving back a single word he could totally commiserate with, **Fuck**.

At home, he was in the spare bedroom they'd transformed into an office for Crissy, staring at the blank screen on the computer. Fingers poised over the keys, he tried to find that thread within himself that had led to here. What he wanted from Po'Boy was the crux of what men like Alcatraz saw as wrong with him, personally. *Looking for porn don't make me a gay boy*.

He sighed and stretched, shaking his hands out. He needed to be in the right mindset for this, and reminded himself, "I'm Ty here. Not Wrench."

"Maybe that's your problem, baby."

He whirled off the chair, wheels rolling it to the side as he crouched, hand to the small of his back where he kept a pistol holstered. Lewis stood in the doorway. Heart racing as he straightened slowly, Ty looked away and blew out a lungful of air, then reached to tug the chair back in front of the desk. Bending at the waist to reach the mouse, he deliberately clicked on the icon to shut the computer down. *Jesus, I'm glad he came in now and not twenty minutes later*. He tried to shake off the subtle feeling of shame that clung to him. *I wasn't doin' anything wrong. Fuck, I wasn't doin' anything yet*. "What are you doin' home, Po'Boy?" He shook his head. "Lewis, I mean."

"Ty, I'm both, man." A hand smoothed up the long muscles of his back to grip the curve where his neck met his shoulders, and fingers dug deep, hitting a nerve that twanged hard down his arm. "You call me whatever you want, I'll always pick up for you. I'm both." Ty shifted sideways as he turned, forcing Lewis' hand to fall away. Much as Lewis had in bed when Ty had his hands on him finally, only to be denied. *And here I am doin' the same damn thing to him*. He closed his eyes to block out the flash of pain on Lewis' face, and his shoulders sagged.

"I know you are. So am I. Just things are...club business. You know how it is." He took a step forwards, blindly seeking out Lewis' heat. "I get stuck in my head." Fingertips glided along his jaw, Lewis wrapping that familiar firm grip around the back of his neck. *This is home.* Ty lifted his hand and followed Lewis' arm until he could touch Lewis' body, flattening his palm and sliding his fingers down until he grazed the front of Lewis' pants. "I don't want to do anything stupid. Not anywhere, but especially there with the club, or here where I lay my head." Lewis moved closer and Ty lifted his chin, hoping for a kiss. He sighed when Lewis rewarded his silent request, lips moving over his gently, teeth plucking at his bottom lip. Lewis' cock swelled under his hand and Ty groaned softly.

"What do you want, Ty?" There it was, the bald ask he'd needed for so long. This was Lewis wanting to make sure he didn't overstep, too, and Ty understood in that moment that they'd both been walking the same path, just on opposite sides of the line.

"I want Crissy home." Lewis' exploration of his mouth paused, then resumed, slower, softer, clearly aiming at a trailing off soon. Ty twisted his neck and put his mouth next to Lewis' ear, not wanting any more misunderstandings to come between them. "She said she wanted to watch the first time you and I were together like I want to be. We both promised her. Cain't go back on a promise, not when she loves her Lewty so much."

"True that," Lewis' breath heated the side of Ty's neck as he bent his head to tease with teeth, biting hard enough to sting. "Damn good thing I called her thirty minutes ago, then, huh?"

"Oh, fuck." He changed his grip on the shaft of Lewis' cock through the fabric, stroking roughly.

"That's the idea, baby." Lewis teased him, then hummed as his hips thrust forwards, pinning Ty's hand between them. "Mmmm. Winner, winner, chicken dinner. Gonna make me blow too soon, you keep that up, lover. Slow and steady, yeah?"

"Well, I'm definitely the winner today." He grabbed hold of Lewis' ass, pulling him tighter as he ground their groins together. "Any way I look at it, I'm winnin' when I'm with you and her."

"We're all winners. Remind me to get our participation ribbons ready." Lewis groaned, his breath coming faster. "Thanks for being here today."

"Thanks for havin' me," he bantered and laughed softly. "Or lettin' me have you."

"Oh, please." Lewis chuckled, his voice low when he asked, "That you tellin' me you're good with either way, no matter how this shakes out?"

Lewis' mouth found Ty's neck again, and he laid a long line of slow, sucking kisses that Ty found himself hoping marked him up good. *I don't give a flyin' shit who sees.* He was surprised with his thought and tried to keep the image of Alcatraz' face from his mind, but the old man clawed his way in. He knew Lewis tagged the change when he slowed, and softly told Ty, "You don't gotta do anything you aren't ready for, baby. Crissy gets here, we can just be whatever we need to be."

"It's weird, people knowing." He'd meant to keep that tucked away, wincing when it escaped his outlaw mouth. Seemed his subconscious was determined to lay bare all his fears today. "I didn't mean that."

"Yeah, you did." Lewis' teeth dug deeply into Ty's shoulder, hands moving over his ribs and back, and Ty wanted skin to skin so badly, just didn't want to move away yet. This felt big, important. "I feel the same."

"You do?" Shocked, he pulled back and found Lewis' staring at him. One corner of his mouth pulled up, but the crooked grin wasn't humorous, more somber and sadder than anything.

"Fuck yeah. Before this—" He reached to tug Ty's shirt up and off, seeming to read his mind. Moving closer, they stood chest to chest, and the heat from Lewis' body washed over him, soothing his nerves. "I kept everything separate. There was club, and there was my suite, and ne're the twain did meet." His Adam's apple bobbed down, disappearing briefly. "I didn't see a way to make things line up how I wanted, so I took what I could from each. Club gave me brothers, my ride or die in Twisted, and my baby chicks with the prospects I mentored. Gave me a reason to breathe every goddamned day, because I was needed there."

Lewis shook his head, thumb grazing a path along Ty's face until he reached his lips, then drifted back and forth there, an endless loop of touch that was also a silent request to not interrupt, to let Lewis get this out. This was theirs, not Crissy's, because as much as she understood the unspoken things society felt about relationships like theirs, she couldn't appreciate the club side. That was a male-dominated aspect of their lives, steeped in rich history and traditions handed down member to member, father to son, and nothing about her life prepared her for the darker sides of things.

She might have ridden to the rescue once, ready to lay waste to the woman hurting Lewis, but she hadn't had to do the deed. And she hadn't risked losing the things that grounded her and made her who she was. Crissy had family who only cared if she was happy, a job that didn't give a shit who she fucked as long as she kept producing for their bottom line, and her friends were their friends, and they also didn't give a shit about how many people cuddled in their bed at night. Lewis and himself, though? *Different story entirely.*

"If Alcatraz has his way, I won't take the gavel from Ace." Even if Lewis wasn't technically CoBos, he had dug so deep into Ty's life, he might as well be. "He's a homophobe, and even after me talking to him today, he said he just can't get behind such a shift in the club. He sees it as a betrayal, what I'm doing with you."

"IMC's lost four members in the past month." Lewis grimaced as he admitted this fact, something Ty hadn't known. "Same reasoning. They're not from chapters around here, all are from one goddammed Texas shithole of a town, which tells me that they've all sucked at the same teat of lies when it comes to me personally." He shrugged. "Shit happens, and we move on."

"We just move on? How? CoBos have just a couple of smaller chapters, and they're so close we do everything together anyway. We lose an OG like Alcatraz, it'll hurt for a long time." He shook his head when Lewis' thumb pressed against his lips. "How do we just move on? How can I let my personal life impact the club like this?"

"You like what we're makin' here, Ty? I know you're good at talkin' the talk, but do you mean it?" Lewis paused and gave him that crooked lift of his lips, then removed his thumb, skating the nail across Ty's cheekbone, fingers threading into his hair. "You seem to like it, but is it deep as it seems for you? Is it worth it, if the worst happens in the club?"

"Yeah, it's deep. This...it's what I want. Wants and needs though?" He huffed out a hard breath. "It feels like I'm being..."

Lewis picked up where Ty had trailed off, nailing what he'd been about to say. "A selfish bastard." This was said without any rancor, no accusation in Lewis' tone. "Right? That's how it feels?" Ty nodded. "That's because for one time in your entire goddamned life you're wantin' to take something just for you. And, I'm standing here, ready to give it. All you gotta do is tell me you want it and

I'm in there, baby. Either way, I'm here and I want you. Because to me, it's not a choice. I want to hold onto the love I feel for you because I'm a better man when we're all together. Not just me and Crissy, but when you're there with us. I want to be good enough to deserve you."

"You already are." Lewis shook his head at Ty's protestation.

"A man's what done things I've done, it ain't no fuckin' given that I'm worth anything. You and me, we're a lot alike in how we've come to where we are, but my path, Ty? Darker than yours. It took me longer to break down the walls. We both got baggage comin' into this. I'm telling you that I don't feel like I deserve the goodness you bring to me." He closed his eyes, features tense with the pain of whatever he was remembering. Ty knew from stories that Lewis' life in the club had started bloody, and stayed that way. After learning about his stepfather and what had happened in the darkness of his childhood, he knew that Lewis' entire life had been him slogging from one field of pain to another. "I want it, though. Want it enough I can nearly catch hold of it, and when I kiss you or kiss our girl, it's that touch, that taste I need."

"You think my best option is to make Ty happy and fuck the club?" He shook his head. "I got responsibilities, man. We both know it."

"So do I." Lewis' eyes opened and he narrowed them as he stared at Ty. "It's not between Ty bein' happy or fuckin' the club over, man. You can have both. You're already both, and...how many members does the CoBos have?"

"Hundred and eleven." Ty knew the exact number because he and Ace had been going over what would shift with the president title. Over the next year, if he were offered the position, he'd be swapping out Ace's officers, and bringing in his own. They'd been settling on the best and most likely candidates for each position today after Ace came over.

"And how many are in danger of walking?"

Ty rolled his eyes as he knew where Lewis was headed. "Ace had the same argument. It's one man, one member, but he's an OG and that counts more. You know that."

"I do, but Ty, listen to yourself. Really listen, and you'll see what I mean. Brother, you got a hundred and ten members standing behind you, and you're tyin' yourself up into fuckin' knots over one man." Lewis straightened, and his eyes hardened, darkening. "Fucking asshole, makin' you doubt yourself like this because he probably was a bitch in prison and can't admit he didn't hate it. Or he hated it so much it tainted his view of everyone like me. Fuck him."

"He has a problem with me, not you."

"That's only because I ain't CoBos, yet. Trust me, he has a problem with me, with who I am. I just don't matter enough in his world yet for him to lay anything out there. That'll change once I patch over."

That statement made Ty pause and stare at Lewis.

"Shut your piehole, man. Ain't an attractive look on you unless you're on your knees for me." Lewis laughed and knuckled Ty's chin up, closing his mouth where it had gawped open. "Don't tell me you hadn't thought on it, because I know I have. There's only one logical choice, which means I'm gonna be the one who moves here, not you."

"Why you?" Ty shifted his stance, pushing one foot backwards as if he were squaring up for a battle and Lewis laughed hard before he twisted his fingers in Ty's hair and yanked his head forwards for a hard, fast kiss that knocked all the fight out of Ty. When Lewis pulled back, Ty braved the sting from his scalp to dart forwards and claim another kiss, that on-demand access something that still felt like magic.

"Because IMC is bigger, and they got folks who can step up and take my place without sending ripples through the organization. I've already talked it over with Twisted and the other officers, so they know it's only a matter of months before I ask to drop my patches honorably."

"Jesus, Lewis. You've been IMC your whole life."

"And you been a CoBo, born and raised." Lewis shrugged. "There aren't any other options for your club if Ace backs away from president. You have strong members, responsible ones who loyally give their backs and strength to the club, but you're the one that's been

77

groomed for this moment. There's no one else, which means if you were to patch over to IMC, Ace has to commit to another decade carrying that weight, training up the next candidate." Lewis tipped his head forwards, resting his forehead against Ty's temple. "You were made to bear the burden, Ty. And I won't make your position weaker because you're sleepin' in the bed of the IMC officer who loves your fuckin' ass. So, I patch over." He shrugged lightly. "As clubs go, we're in each other's pockets all the time anyway. Look at your old apartment complex for example. Half the units are your club, the other half's mine. It'd keep the CoBos independent longer, too. I know my worth, baby. I do bring something to the table, and I will have your goddamned back in anything that goes down. Wearing the same patch makes that a fuckton easier, and you and I both know it."

"Well, when you put it like that." He snorted. "Sounds like a done deal, and one I'd be stupid to turn down."

"And you ain't a stupid man. Choosin' me shows just how smart you are." Lewis sighed. "Won't be without bumps, but knowin' you're here for me helps."

And with those words, Lewis managed to settle something in Ty's chest. *He needs me just like I need him.* "I've been an ass. I didn't realize you would fight the same battles inside."

"Not an ass." Lewis' cheek creased as he smiled, and Ty grinned to see it, knowing that whatever came out of his mouth next would move the conversation back to where they'd begun. He was not wrong. "You do have quite the ass, though. It's one I've become acquainted with quite well over the past bit, but I have to admit, baby, I wanna know it…intimately."

"You've already breached those bulwarks." Ty rolled his eyes. "That was terrible. Almost as bad as your quip about backdoor bliss, which I have not forgotten."

"Yeah, but why's it stickin' in your headbone, man? Because it was bad, or because the thought of it was so damned good?" There was that sly grin, and Ty fell a little more in love with this asshole in that moment. *He's my asshole.*

"You are somethin' else, Ralph Lewis." He shook his head, glad when Lewis' grip moved to the back of his neck again, because something about that hold was always so steadying; it set the framework for the freedom he needed to be able to say what he wanted. "I want it all, Lewis. I know you think I don't, or that it'll fuck me up, but it's never been us that did that. It was the club and me bein' afraid of losing what I'd been existing for there. Existing, not livin'. There's a difference, and you feel it too. Makes me want to fight for us even more, knowin' you're beatin' back the same demons. Now you say you're patching over, and that means I can't lose it. You've got my back, and I'll be able to have yours, too. Just having that settled in my mind makes it so I'm content now." He pressed closer, fingernails of one hand scratching for entrance across the fabric at Lewis' crotch. Rucking up the hem of his tee, Ty placed his other hand on Lewis' back, strong muscles there moving like water under the supple skin. "I want it all. Can you give that to me?"

Lewis didn't respond, said not a word as he took Ty's hand, fingers curling around his in a firm hold, tugging him towards their bedroom. Anticipation quivered through Ty's belly, setting his hands shaking and he knew Lewis felt it when he paused and pushed Ty against the wall, stripping his own shirt off as he stared into Ty's eyes, his hair wild around his face. Then they were chest to chest, and Lewis was devouring him, breaking him apart with a kiss that didn't hold back, showing all the desire that had been dammed up inside. Ty met him stroke for stroke, gasping into Lewis' mouth when fingers unfastened his jeans, one hand slipping in the front, one the back, both gripping and pulling, touching in different ways until he was dizzy with need. Cheeks stretched apart, the chill of air hitting his hole was counterpoint to the hot palm stroking his dick. When Lewis stepped back and looked at him, head tipped to one side, he wore a crooked grin that Ty wanted to kiss off his face as he realized what his lover had done.

"I'm good," he promised, and Lewis nodded.

"Better'n good, you're fuckin' tasty. Gonna get me another mouthful here in a minute." Leading the way down the hallway again, Lewis flashed a glance over his shoulder towards the outside door. "She made it just in time." They didn't slow, Lewis' grip on his hand firm, implacable as the door opened. Ty heard the familiar thump of Crissy's shoes hitting the mat just beside the entryway table, then the soft echo of her bare feet hurrying their direction.

"Hey." Fingers hooked in his belt loops and she laughed when she nearly took the loose pants to his midthigh. "This is a good look for you."

"Hey, baby," he said. He yanked his pants back up, then held his arm out in invitation. She skipped up beside him and cuddled close so he could wrap her up tight. "Good to see you." Lewis tugged on his hand and Ty looked up to see him walking backwards, smiling. "What did Lewis say when he called you?"

Crissy giggled and pressed her cheek to his chest. "Told me he wanted to play."

"That's all it took to get you outta work early?" Ty was surprised because she was dedicated to her job, attacking each day as if she still had to earn her way onto the graphics team at the ad agency where she worked. "Damn, I been slackin'."

"He's never called before, so I knew whatever he wanted to *play*," she gave air quotes around the word with one hand, "had to be good. I dropped everything, didn't give a reason for leaving, just hooked it out of there fast as I could."

"I'm glad you're here." He kissed the side of her head, pausing while Lewis opened the bedroom door. "We made you a promise a few weeks ago. I told him we couldn't break that promise."

"Oh, yeah?" She pulled away from him and went to Lewis, rolling far up on her toes to offer him her lips. Ty watched as they kissed, lost in each other within moments, eyes closed as their heads angled, mouths working against the other with soft sounds.

"Yeah," he whispered. "A promise is a promise, after all."

Lewis broke free first, heavy-lidded eyes lifting to Ty's face. "In that case, I promise to give you everything you want, Ty."

Crissy had folded against Lewis' chest, arms tucked in front of her, held there with Lewis' arm. "What'd you ask for, Ty?" She turned her head and gave him a sidelong glance, the apple of her cheek lifting with her tiny smile, the one she kept close and only used when she was happiest. "Hmmm?"

Things he couldn't say aloud to Lewis earlier bubbled out of him, a result of the kiss in the hallway coupled with watching these two people he loved make out as they had, freed his tongue and he laid everything out there. *No excuses after this*. "I want Lewis to take me from behind while I'm inside you, wanna feel him moving behind me, in me, while you're under me takin' everything I have. That's a long-term goal." He gave a ghost of a grin, pushing through to the end. "But today, right now, I want to know that he wants me. I wanna be something he can't get anywhere else, not anymore. I want to blow his mind, and fuck his ass however he wants, and I want you to be right there with us. Fingers and tongue and pussy, all mixed in with ass and cock."

"That's a big order, Ty. We're gonna need a stretch of time for all of that." Crissy grinned at him. "Lewis, thank God you called when you did."

"Come into my lair." Lewis leered and drew both of them into the bedroom. "Ty, I wanna see your hands behind your head. Get 'em out of the way, because me and Crissy...this is our show right now."

There wasn't much left to undress on him, but Lewis and Crissy made a meal out of it. Ty stood, fingers clasped behind his head as ordered, giving up command for at least this portion of the night. Crissy was on her knees in front of him, tongue laving across his belly, stopping to nip and bite as she went. Her hands were on the seams of his jeans, tugging them slowly down his legs in deliberately teasing movements. Ty shuffled his feet out slightly to tighten the fabric across his thighs, wanting to slow her down because he needed to focus on what Lewis was doing, and if she got to his cock too soon, he knew he'd be lost.

There was the rustle of fabric from behind, then Lewis was against him, molded to his back, hard cock thrusting against his ass. Mouth fastened to Ty's shoulder, Lewis moved and shifted, each rolling change in position giving them more skin-on-skin contact. Guided by Crissy's fingers, the waistband of his jeans slipped lower, and Ty gave it up, letting them fall as far as Crissy wanted. Lewis' hips pulled away, then his cock was prodding between Ty's cheeks, angled down and bumping low, thrusting in a slow rhythm between his thighs. "Oh, yeah, you were ready for this." Lewis slapped his bare ass and made Ty jump, which made Crissy giggle. "He's commando, girlie, and I do love a man with confidence like that."

Hard fingers skated along his ribs, slowly tracing every bump and ridge. A calloused palm slipped low on Ty's belly, pulling him back firmly against Lewis' pumping hips. Ty tipped his chin up, tightening his fingers' grip in his hair hard as a reminder to be still while Crissy wrestled his jeans to the floor. She had him lift his legs in turn, one hand stroking his cock. Her hair brushed lightly at the join of his leg and hip, and he heard a wet sound that came and went in time with Lewis' thrusts. Looking down, he watched as she lapped at the end of Lewis' cock as it made a brief appearance between his thighs, sucking for as long as it was visible.

"*Fuuuck.*"

Hunger and desire filled her expression when she looked up. With one hand, she angled his cock down and let it slide between her lips the next time Lewis pushed his hips forwards. Now Ty was trapped between them, Lewis' body behind him moving both of them in turn, and Crissy in front, letting them fuck her face with Ty's cock. Work roughened fingertips twisted his nipple, and he hissed, then Lewis' mouth was at his ear, and one of his favorite parts of any session with the two of them began.

Voice low and rough, Lewis' words flowed across Ty, giving him a glimpse of the man's desire. "See our Crissy lovin' you? You see that, Ty? She's takin' everything you want to give her. Feed that dick into her mouth, baby. She loves it like that." Lewis' other hand appeared in view, fingers threading through Crissy's hair, gently holding her head still as he increased the pace and motion of his thrusts against Ty's ass. "Fucking her face, baby. That's you and me, we're deep in it now. Suck his knob, Crissy girl, get it sloppy for me. Make it easy for me to sit on in a fast minute. Want his cock in my ass so *bad*. He's gonna give it to me good, and I can't wait." Ty groaned, and Lewis chuckled. "Oh, yeah, he's into all of this. Jesus, you're so beautiful, Crissy. Lovin' on our Ty like this."

Lewis shoved Ty deep, and Crissy gagged and choked, harsh sounds coming from her. But true to form, her hands flew to cup the back of Ty's legs to hold his dick in place when Lewis would have pulled back. Now she was fighting Lewis' grip on her hair, trying to take Ty even deeper. "*Jesus*, Crissy." Ty felt and saw her swallow, the back of her throat closing around the tip of his dick, compressing tightly around him, the muscles working to pull him deeper. He heaved back against Lewis, pulling out of Crissy's mouth, leaving her gasping for a moment before she yanked him forwards again. "Baby, stop it. I'm gonna come."

Lewis released her, hand smoothing down the side of her face. "Pull off, Crissy. I want it from him. Give me this one, darlin'."

She drew back, keeping her tongue at work along the sides of Ty's shaft, causing zings of electricity to jolt through his body, toes to groin, groin to belly, belly to brain. Fingers tingling, he curled one hand around Lewis' arm across his chest, the other going to grip Crissy's slippery chin between finger and thumb.

"So fuckin' good, honey. You make me feel like the king of the world. I love when you want me like that." He angled her face up and pulled in a breath, hoping she could see in his expression how much he adored her. "Luckiest man on earth." Mouth swollen, she smiled up at him, tongue coming out to lick along her lips. "Love you, Crissy."

"Love you, too," she whispered back.

"Bed, now." Lewis' voice was rough, filled with gravel. It rattled through Ty's chest from where they were pressed together, and he groaned when Lewis pulled from between his thighs, the slick left behind the testimony to how much Lewis had been enjoying himself. "On your back, lover."

Ty crawled onto the mattress, flipping to his back as ordered, and looked up at Lewis where he stood statue-still at the foot of the bed. Crissy slipped onto the sheets next to him, her clothes having vanished somewhere along the way. He cupped a breast, lifting and caressing her, thumb roughing up her nipple before soothing with a gentler stroke. Lewis was breathing hard and fast, and Ty saw his hands clench into fists, then open as he smoothed them down his own thighs. "Lewis?"

"God, the dirty, dirty things I want to do to you, Tyler Sawyer. I want to fuck your ass, hear you calling out for me to hit your button again, and again. Wanna take your cock hard, give you a ride you'd never forget, Crissy sucking me off as we came, you inside my ass, her mouth on me giving me what she gave you just now. I wanna eat you raw, fuck you with my tongue while Crissy rides my cock. So many things we have waiting for us, Ty. And *I* get them. I get it all, with you. You and our Crissy make all my dreams come true."

Ty lifted both hands and curled his fingers in a "come on" gesture, following it up with a voice he hoped didn't shake. "Bring it, baby."

Lewis tongued the inside of his cheek as he shook his head slowly, then he put a knee on the edge of the mattress, hands to both Ty's ankles as he yanked them to the sides of the bed, putting Ty on display. When the chill air hit his balls, he shivered, and Lewis chuckled. "You know how good you look?"

Ty shook his head.

"I could—" He dipped his chest to the covers, wedging Ty's thighs wide with his shoulders. "—eat you all up. Gorge myself on all of you."

"Yeah?" Ty was still trying for some level of nonchalant, even knowing he was losing that battle quickly. "Eat me, then."

"That's what she said," Crissy mumbled and then shook with quiet laughter. "Sorry, sorry. I'll be quiet."

"Don't be quiet, Crissy girl." Lewis scraped the inside of Ty's thigh with either his nails or teeth. Ty's head was shoved so far back into the pillow he couldn't see anything except the insides of his eyelids. "Be bold."

She moved, head resting on Ty's chest. "Bold?"

Another scrape and this was definitely teeth, because it was followed by a hard suck, higher on his leg, Lewis' cheek stubble rasping against his sac. "Yeah, bold. Be you, sweet girl. Ty?" He answered with a grunt. "You hungry, baby?"

"God, yes." Ty brought his head up, reaching for Crissy's shoulders. "Come here and feed me, yeah?" She stared at him a moment, then scrambled to get her knees underneath her, Lewis laughing at the eagerness with which she responded to their blatant suggestion. She looked confused when he steered her to straddle his chest facing Lewis but relaxed when he told her, "You wanted to watch."

"That she did. Good call there, Ty. I'll be sure to give our girl a show." He couldn't see Lewis now but had a grand view of Crissy's heart-shaped ass, her strong back arching over him. He could feel Lewis, though, every movement slow and deliberate, bringing Ty closer to what he wanted. Lewis had sucked him off before, but that was normally either in tandem with Crissy or during cleanup after playtime, one of Lewis' favorite parts. So when Lewis shoved a hand under Ty's knees and lifted, he moved as directed, heels set far to each side. "Need some room to work, baby. I'm nearly ready, you get started up there. You and Crissy, y'all gotta do the same. Gotta put on a show for me."

There was the click of a lid, and then something cool drizzled on his cock. That didn't make sense, because if Lewis was going to suck him off, he surely wouldn't want the taste of lube to begin the evening. Shaking his head, Ty gripped Crissy's hips and lifted, pulling her backwards until she was poised over his face, pussy lips glistening in the low light, her rich, musky scent engulfing him. "God, you smell so good. Wet? Fuck yeah. You liked suckin' on me, didn't you?" He raised his chin and then lapped at her, starting at the clit and pulling back to her entrance where he teased with the tip of his tongue. From this angle, he'd be able to travel across every sensitive inch and planned on doing things to her until she was screaming his name, or her version of their names. Ty suppressed a chuckle. "Oh, Lewty," he murmured as a tease, licking along her seam again, lapping deep to pull her taste into his mouth. "Oh, please, Lewty."

Ty alternated between diving deep, thrusting and wiggling his tongue as far as he could reach into her slick pussy, and dragging his teeth and chin across her clit. Building her slowly, he urged her to move as she desired, his hands lifting, then pulling on her ass to slide her across his face. Then came the first slow stroke on his cock, and it had him pulling in air with a hiss because it felt so good. He'd been hard since before he and Lewis started their walk up the hallway, and it was a relief to be touched like this, knowing more was coming. The lube made for a slippery surface, each rock of his hips setting him through Lewis' fist on a smooth glide.

Then something touched his hole and he clenched up momentarily, the reaction instinctive. "Not a bad touch, baby." Lewis' voice was smooth as velvet, surrounding Ty with the silky tones, seductive and just so goddamned familiar it took his breath away. "This is gonna be so good."

Crissy made an impatient sound, and he realized he'd frozen midlick. Reclaiming his previous rhythm seemed impossible, but he found a new one, catching his stride with licking and sucking, rocking his hips up as Lewis stroked him steadily. The touch turned into pressure, Lewis' mouth on his thigh, teeth digging in firmly as he pushed a finger into Ty. "God, yes."

Chapter Seven

Lewis

Ty cried out, voice soft and warbling with desire and the tiniest bit of fear. Lewis lifted his gaze to Crissy's face, her eyes were closed, chin drawn down to her chest as she rocked back and forth over Ty's face, the sound of him eating her loud and obscene, gloriously carnal. He loved them like this, raw and unfiltered, when they showed him everything.

His hand stripped Ty's cock with a carefully firm grip. For what he was going to do, he didn't want Ty too excited but needed to keep him riding the edge of pleasure. Thick and long, the crown was mushroomed out, Ty's dick angry red and jerking in his grip, the slit giving him a steady supply of fluid to supplement the small amount of lube he'd used.

Lewis dropped his gaze to where his fingertip had breached Ty's asshole to the second knuckle, nearly enough to stroke his prostate. He laid his mouth in alongside his hand, licking around his finger again, wetting everything he could touch with his tongue. *In just a little further*. He found the edges of the small spongy gland and touched it gently. Ty gasped and groaned, the muscles of his legs shaking with the effort it took to keep them spread wide. Lewis looked up to see Crissy staring at him, mouth open as she breathed fast, watching. Out, and then back in, with another careful touch and stroke, and Ty shouted, the barked sound inarticulate and wild.

The sounds of him feasting on Crissy redoubled, and she rolled her lips between her teeth, biting down to stay quiet. Ty brought a hand around Crissy's legs, fingers stroking along the cherry red clit Lewis could see peeking out from her lips. She groaned again, the tone deeper, more guttural and he knew that sound. That was Crissy's tell for assplay, which she liked a lot. *Nearly as much as I do*. He again stroked back and grazed Ty's gland with a brief touch, then withdrew his finger, licking and playing with Ty's hole, giving the man a chance to get Crissy off. There was a deliberate focus to the sounds coming from that end of the bed, and Lewis recognized Ty was fighting to hold off a climax himself. If he could concentrate on either of his lovers, Ty could back off from the edge again and again, and tonight that was just fine with Lewis.

"Crissy." She looked hazy when she opened her eyes, and Lewis smiled. *That's a good look on her.* She blinked owlishly. "Ty treatin' you good, honey?" She nodded, curls of hair dancing alongside her breasts. "Sweet Crissy mine, I got a question for you. You listenin'?"

Ty's hand moved, and she gasped, then whispered through clenched teeth, "Yes."

"Sweet Crissy, our bold girl. Can I fuck you?"

She blinked and opened her mouth, but the only sound that came out was a rising cry of, "Ty."

"Give it to her good, baby. She tastes so good, I know, you wanna eat your fill, but I got plans for the night. Bring it home, and then let me in there." He tightened his hand around Ty's cock, still stroking steadily, but now the rim of the head bumped against his fingers with every pass up and down. Wetting Ty's hole again, he slowly pushed in two fingers, moving at a glacier's pace to get deep enough. Then he was able to set up a scissoring rhythm inside, keeping constant touch against the nerve-clustered gland, first one finger, then the other, then the first again, using a familiar curling motion. Crissy called out and sat upright, hands lifting to her breasts, fingers pinching each nipple, pulling them taut and twisting.

"I'm coming," she panted, and Ty's chest rose and fell along with hers. Lewis could just see his jaw opening and throat quivering. "Oh, Lewis, Ty." Another gasp of air, then she whimpered, "Please."

Lewis pushed to his knees, hands continuing to move on and in Ty as he bent forwards. "Kiss me, beautiful." She did, body rising and falling with each new assault Ty made on her pussy, mouth working against Lewis' frantically. She froze and keened, and Lewis changed gears so he could put his arms around her, holding her upright as the orgasm wracked her body with rolling shudders. He straddled Ty's hips, not realizing how things had lined up until the head of Ty's cock brushed his ass. *Not yet*. With a bow of his back, he moved so their cocks lay on Ty's belly, side by side, and the next time Ty lifted his hips, his cock glided along Lewis'. *Little frotwork never hurt anybody*.

"Enough," she shouted, lifting off Ty's face only to be yanked back down by his hands at her hips. "Ty, enough. It's too much."

When she rose to her knees again, Ty's hands slipped up her back to curl around Lewis' wrists. Looking over her shoulder, he saw Ty's eyes were glassy, his face wet and shining as he smiled up. "Hey."

"Hey, yourself," Lewis returned. "Lemme get her laid down. Gotta take care of our girl, yeah?" Ty nodded, the smile on his face not dimming a bit. "You enjoyed that?"

"Oh, yeah. I liked that. In case you couldn't tell." Ty's hips rose and his cock slapped against Lewis' belly. "I liked it all."

A moment later and he had Crissy on her side next to Ty, her arm across his chest while Lewis kissed him soundly, taking in the musky taste of Crissy from his lips. When Ty reached for him, he backed off and went for a wet cloth. He didn't want to touch Crissy's pussy yet, because with as wet as she was, he'd enjoy fucking her without a cleanup there. But he suspected once Ty came down from the high of what they'd done so far, he'd rather his face not be flooded with her juices.

When he got back to the bed, Crissy and Ty had swapped places, Crissy now on her back. Ty's hand was between her legs, idly playing with her and Lewis grinned at the idea of Ty keeping her revved up for him. He bent down and kissed Crissy softly, wiped her face with the warm cloth, then did the same for Ty. Scanning the bed, he didn't see the bottle anywhere, so he looked on the floor.

"Whatcha lookin' for?" He glanced up at the question to find Ty was dangling the bottle between his fingers, a grin on his face.

"That, asshole."

"I'll take care of your asshole, baby."

Lewis tried not to preen, but he loved when either of them called him a pet name. Baby being one of his personal favorites. "Promises, promises." He reused a taunt from the other night, and Ty showed teeth in a slightly feral smile.

"Crissy's ready for you." Ty spread her labia and Lewis watched as his middle finger slid into her effortlessly, pushing far inside, the tendons in Ty's wrist standing out with the strain as he tried for another inch, grinding deep. She mewled as he withdrew, hips lifting, a shudder rolling through her when he painted the juices across her clit. "She's ready, baby."

The look of anticipation on Ty's face as he spoke showed he'd marked the previous reaction to the word, and Lewis gladly gave it to him again, letting him see how much he liked it. Liked being worth the kinds of pet names that came with familiarity. The kind of comfort that came from knowing you were going to be with someone long term. Smiling, proud of the heady relationship he was part of, he stared at Ty as he said, "I'm ready, too. What a co-inky-dink."

With an expression of sublime happiness, Ty closed his eyes and rolled his head towards Crissy and sucked on her nipple, taking as much of her breast in his mouth as he could. His fingers still held her pussy open, and Lewis wasted no time in sliding into place, hips notching into the cradle made just for them. He didn't shy from Ty's touch, didn't pull away as he had over the past weeks, letting his cock slide up past her entrance and over Ty's hand, then back down. Fingers gripped him, hot, wrapping all the way around his shaft. He gasped as Ty lined him up with Crissy's opening and then Lewis rocked his hips forwards, plunging inside by a measured amount. "Nearly too much," he warned Ty when the fingers didn't abandon their hold, instead changing to a two-fingered stroke. At his warning, Ty curled a finger around the base of Lewis' sac, pressing on his taint. "Fuck," he gasped as his hips bucked hard. "Not helping."

Crissy laughed, and Lewis shook his head. That was a sound he loved hearing from her, especially in bed, a place where she'd once been cautious. *We broke her of that*. He smirked down at them, wishing he could freeze frame this moment. Crissy's eyes on him, fingers in Ty's hair holding him to her breast, his eyes closed as he sucked and played, his shoulder in view with muscles bunched. Soft and hard, strong and stronger. "Y'all are mine, you know that, right?" Crissy grinned and nodded, Ty's eyes opening and cutting up and to the side so he could look at Lewis without releasing his mouth-hold on her tit. "Mine," Lewis said, hips shoving forwards to drive him deeper inside her on a slow glide. Retreat, then stroke in again. "Mine."

He grunted when the grip on him constricted and released as Ty pushed up to an elbow, moving up to face Crissy. Watching them kiss while he moved in and out of her was one of the best feelings. Ty cupped her cheeks protectively, possessively, taking her mouth with a gentle intensity Lewis could feel radiating off the man. It curled his toes like an orgasm, knowing they cherished each other as much as he did them, and he started bucking harder, trying to balance Ty's soft and sweet with a little fast fucking. Best way to get her brain to let go.

97

With Lewis propped up on his arms like this, it gave Ty plenty of room to touch and caress, hand cradling her breast, fingers pinching the still-wet nipple until her pussy gave a rippling squeeze around Lewis. Her legs spread farther, then her heels came up behind his ass, her hips lifting to meet every thrust. Crissy had one hand still wrapped around Ty's skull, fingers in his hair, but her other hand lifted to touch Lewis' chest, gliding up until she had a similar hold on him. For such a little thing, she was strong, and he gave in quickly as she tugged him down. Ty shifted to the side, and Lewis kissed her, tongue chasing hers for a moment. Her grip changed and she turned his head towards their lover as Ty moved in, and he was kissing Ty, giving way to the greediness of his caress, Ty taking control, biting his lips, sucking his tongue until Lewis gasped out, "*Baby*," head swimming from the sensations of Crissy hot and tight around his dick, Ty's mouth owning him until all he could think was a string of *love, love, love, this is love*.

He lost Crissy's legs around him. A hand on his ass was all the warning he needed to slow and push deep, muscles clenching hard for a moment in heady anticipation before he consciously relaxed as much as he could. Lube-slick, Ty's finger delved between his cheeks and aimed unerringly towards his hole, slipping inside effortlessly as Lewis pushed out. Ty grunted when Lewis clenched, showing him how tight and hot it would be once he was really inside. Then Lewis eased up, released the taut hold on Ty's digit and buried his head beside Crissy's in the pillow, waiting.

Ty didn't disappoint, plunging and twisting, dragging against the muscles as he withdrew before adding a second finger, the burn a quiet promise of what would be Lewis' very soon. In and out, deeper and deeper, giving Lewis the full width of his fingers before he added a third. "Fuck, Ty. So goddamned good."

"You need more?" Ty's mouth was right beside Lewis' ear, the rough words coming out on a gust of heated breath, followed by a low groan when Lewis shook his head. "You sure, baby. I don't want to hurt you."

Baby. God, he'd kill to keep hearing that word from Ty. "I'm sure. Christ yes, I'm sure, I'm sure."

The mattress moved and Crissy held him tight, as if he'd run away from this, but he knew what she meant by her actions. "I love you, honey doll. Love you."

"I love you, too, big man." She kissed the side of his head until he turned to face her, their noses a scarce span apart. Lewis puckered his lips and grazed her mouth, capturing her breath. The plastic cap clicked again, and then he heard Ty stroking himself, the lube making a distinctive sound that ratcheted up his desire. "Your face." Crissy touched his cheek, and he blinked to focus back on her. "You really want this." He nodded, words lost for the moment. "Ty, be good to our Lewis, yeah?" She adopted the cadence Lewis had often used when he coached his lovers. "Love him good. He wants this so bad, lover. Wants you, and I know you know it. I've seen you watch him, caught how you stare. Be good to each other, and I'll promise you it will be the best, ever. Lewis—" She smiled and kissed his nose. "—thank you for being the other part of my soul."

"Nothing to thank me for, honey." He returned her gesture, pressing his lips to the tip of her nose. He offered honesty with his whispered, "I live and breathe for the two of you."

Furred legs pushed his thighs farther apart and he shifted, vigilant to stay deep inside Crissy. Then Ty's bare dick nudged his hole, scalding as it pressed relentlessly forwards, pushing and prodding, and he carefully bore down again, as he had for Ty's fingers, rewarded when the crown of Ty's monster cock slipped inside. Ty hissed and froze, sounding shocked when he said, "Hotter than I expected, oh man. Jesus. *Fucking*...it's sexy as fuck, watching me go inside you, baby."

He groaned as Ty palmed both globes of his ass, thumbs running between and then Lewis tensed as they were tugged apart so Ty could give himself a clearer field of view. Lewis knew what Ty'd see. A taut ridge of muscle encircling his cock, the gleam of oil on the shaft, shining smears of the lubricant on Lewis' skin. Ty forced himself deeper, and Lewis arched his back, muscles of his neck contracting as his head lifted.

"Feels so good, Ty. So fuckin' good."

Crissy's palms soothed up and down his arms as she dusted kisses across his shoulder. "You feel good, I feel good, I think Ty feels good."

"Ty definitely feels good," Ty muttered, "I'm afraid to move, Lewis. It's more...I didn't expect it to be this."

"Hmm." Lewis was reeling, drunk as he brought his lips down to capture Crissy's. "I got you, baby boy. You be still, let good old Lewis do all the work." He made a tentative shift of his hips and chuckled when both Crissy and Ty gasped in unison as they pulled in a quick breath. It took a minute, but he found his stride, a slow back and forth that had Ty sliding in and out of his ass inches at a time, and his cock driving deep into Crissy before withdrawing again. And again. "Fucking hot and tight, and havin' Ty fucking me is the best. Best. Been waitin' for this, worth every minute, baby. Worth it all." Sweat slicked his skin, dripping into his eyes, heat from Ty's legs on his thighs a furnace that was linked by him to Crissy's burn from underneath. The room filled with a chorus of groans and moans, Ty cursing under his breath, fingers digging into Lewis' ass and hips with a painful desperation he welcomed. *Gonna be marked up so good tomorrow*. Crissy was writhing, hips coming up to meet every thrust, legs moving restlessly. "We still all fine?"

"Mmhmm, so fine," Crissy hummed softly, head turning to the side, hair shielding her face from him. The way she was panting hard, he knew she was close, and with how he'd been using Ty's cock to stroke his own prostate, he'd come with her when she locked down on him.

"Ty, baby, you with us?" A jolting thud of Ty's hips against his ass was his answer, and Lewis arched his head around, staring over his shoulder at the man behind him. Ty was looking down, eyes fixed on where they were joined, but he was moving in counterpoint to Lewis now, meeting him in the middle with a delicious hard thrust. "Oh, yeah, you're with us." Lewis was the fulcrum their movement tied to, and he increased the pace, then held that rhythm, giving Ty a chance to get caught up before he sped up again. "I'm gonna go deep, Ty. Deep as I can inside Crissy and I want you to follow me down. Lean on me, lay on me, do whatever you need to do, but fuck me, baby. Fuck me hard. Fuck me into our Crissy."

He lowered his chest until Crissy's breasts brushed against him with every plunge inside her. Ass slightly cocked up into the air, he stretched out one leg, using the other to lift Crissy's knee wide. Once back in the position they'd started in, he rocked hard, grinding against her clit while Ty came down on his shaking arms. Keeping the hard dick deep in his ass, Lewis maintained the delicate rocking motion, giving Ty a moment to get used to the dynamics of their new positions. Hand on his shoulder, Ty pulled Lewis back against him before thrusting hard. Crissy grunted in surprise, mouth open in a soundless shout at the power behind the movement.

"Gonna go hard, Lewis. I can't…I want to go hard, gotta."

"Fuck me, Ty. Fuck me and fuck Crissy. Do it." Ty's nails dug into the skin under Lewis' collarbone and he readied himself. "Do it."

He'd seen Ty fuck Crissy, seen him make love to her, too. Watched and participated with both. But nothing had prepared him for the sheer, overwhelming power of Ty's body, muscles pulling and pushing fast and hard, the broad shaft of Ty's cock thrusting into him. Taking him to the root like that set the burn in his ass blazing again, and Lewis' embraced it, breathing through the long push of Ty's thick shaft that took forever to hit bottom, and then another forever to pull out until the head was all that remained inside him, before Ty slammed into him, starting the whole movement all over again.

Ty took Lewis apart, and turned him out, striking his gland directly for a few strokes, then deliberately twisting his hips to graze along the edges, dragging a low groan of frustration from Lewis. The whole time, the hand not being used for leverage was dancing across Lewis' skin, nails dragging at his nipple then down his side, palm in a long stroke up his spine, then positioned between his shoulder blades to firmly shove him down another inch so Ty could gain greater advantage. Lewis' throat burned from his shouts, and Ty met each with guttural responses, giving him filthy promise after promise, and all Lewis could think was "Please, God. Please."

"I got you, baby." Ty grunted and turned up the speed another notch. "I got you both."

Crissy lifted and bent her knees to cradle Lewis' hips, her pelvis angled so he went deeper, the violence of Ty's thrusts causing their flesh to slap together, creating the perfect percussion. Lewis dipped his neck and kissed her, biting her bottom lip before he released and sucked it hard, tongue fucking her mouth. "Ty," she cried, then "Lewis, Ty."

"Awww, there she goes, Ty baby." She clenched around him, legs quivering as she gripped tight to him, holding on. "We got us a Lewty." She keened, high and shrill, sounding desperate as she lifted her hands to the top of her head, fingers twisting in her own hair. "Fuck yeah, doll. Take yours." She rolled under him, hips and belly and back joining into a dance that drove him wild, and Lewis knew he was done for. "Comin', baby. Comin' so fuckin' hard." His hips stuttered, jittering back and forth as if undecided, then his body took over and stiffened, driving deep as the end of his cock exploded, heat and the tightness of her sheath drawing his orgasm out long and hard. "Fuck, fuck, fuck," he chanted, forehead dropping to her shoulder. "Comin' so hard."

Pulses of heat filled him as Ty lurched in place, hips still pistoning fast. Ty's hand dropped from Lewis' shoulder to his hip, tight grip of his fingers now certain to leave marks, and Lewis knew he'd look at them every day until they faded, loving the way they made him feel. Possessed, and owned, and loved. Ty's chest hit his back, sweat-slick skin sliding easily, then his teeth were worrying at the flesh over his shoulder blade, Ty latching on hard through a yell that sounded so proud and victorious it made Lewis preen all over again. "Fuck me, Lewis. So good, baby. You're so good."

"We're good," Crissy slurred the words, sounding half asleep already. "Cleanup in aisle three."

Ty laughed, and Lewis felt it, felt the roll of the music as it pushed through him, rattling against the overworked nerves of his ass.

"So fucking good," Ty grunted, his arms bracketing Lewis, biceps trembling with the strain as he pushed himself up.

"Well, you're so good at fucking." Lewis waited and was rewarded by another laugh. Ty slid slowly from his ass, and Lewis smiled down at Crissy as he felt lips trail down his back, pressing into first one cheek, then the other. "What's that for?"

"That sweet, sweet ass." Ty flung himself to the mattress beside Crissy, tipping her face towards him with a fingertip on her cheek, tracing along the curve of her jaw. "You are amazing, sweetheart." He looked up at Lewis, then shifted to the side, creating space. "Get down here, baby. We needa nap before round two."

Chapter Eight
Lewis

Ace was waiting for him when Po'Boy walked through the door. To be expected, since he'd called ahead of time and set up this conversation. Wrench knew in some vague way that Po'Boy planned on chatting with the current CoBos president, but his fella didn't know it was today, something Po'Boy knew he'd pay for later. *Maybe Ty'll take it outta my ass.* He didn't try to stifle the smirk that chased across his lips, keeping secrets from the man in front of him who wouldn't have any idea what it was for.

"Po'Boy," Ace called, standing and reaching for Po'Boy's outstretched hand. "Welcome. Want a beer?"

Without waiting on a response, Ace called across the room. "Bring two cold ones to the office." Turning back to Po'Boy, he said, "Walk with me."

Ace opened the office door and led the way, giving Po'Boy a chance to look around. The table was etched with the Caddo Hobos patch, looking to have been carved into the wood with pocket knives, faint blade marks still apparent along the edges. Legend had it the founders threw an epic party and one member began the process, which continued for days as each patch brother laid a blade to the table used for church. A lasting way to score their mark on the club they loved. The walls held a flag of the club's colors, an American flag, and a POW flag. Everything as expected. What was surprising was the video conference set-up on a side table and a wall-mounted TV.

"Y'all goin' high tech? Nice." Po'Boy pulled out a chair along the side of the table, intending to leave his back to the door in an overt sign of respect he knew Ace would note and appreciate.

"Retro recommended a guy. His brother's club's got a tech wizard, and I figured if I had a resource, might as well take advantage of it. We're in the process of setting up every member with an app, so if I need them, I can get them. It's a private network thing." He shrugged and laughed. "Not a fucking thing of it that I understand, but I'm told it's nearly impossible for even the Feds to break into it. I'm down for that kind of cockblocking anytime."

Ace remained standing, and Po'Boy paused, holding his place, waiting.

The prospect scurried in and dropped the two bottles on the edge of the table nearest Po'Boy before turning and leaving, closing the door behind him. Po'Boy studied the door, then looked at the beers and finally glanced up at Ace to see him grinning broadly. "What the fuck's the matter with him?" He picked up a bottle and held it out to Ace, who took it with a laugh.

"I suspect he's a little awed at being in the company of the infamous Po'Boy." Ace kicked a chair out at the end of the table and sat, and Po'Boy settled into his chosen seat.

"The fuck you say?" He waited until Ace had sipped from his bottle before doing the same. Another intentional sign of respect he hoped would move some tokens over to his jar of favors. *With what I'm asking, I'm gonna need all the help I can get.*

"No shit, man. You are the *talk* of the club these days. Every time I turn around, folks are askin' about you." Ace shrugged. "I play it up. See how far I can drag things out." Po'Boy laughed. "How's things in IMC land?"

"Good. Surprisingly good, considering everything that went down happened so recent." He decided to stop beating around the bush and get to business. "You know why I'm here?"

"I have my suspicions." Ace shrugged. "Why don't you lay it out for me, so there's no misunderstandings. I'd hate to find out later I got anything wrong."

"Talked to Twisted last week about this. He ain't happy, but he gets it. I talked until he understood. Everything begins and ends in this room, Ace. You've made no secret about your succession plan here with the CoBos. My goal is to not get in the way of that, because it's what you need, and it's what Wrench wants." He thumped the table with the tip of one finger. "I like where I live, like the people here in the region. I like to keep things...stable. CoBos being solid helps keep everything copasetic for all of us."

"Ain't your only reason." Ace narrowed his eyes as he sipped his beer. "Lay it out there, Po'Boy. You ain't gonna shock me."

"One of my biggest arguments against Twisted takin' Penny to his bed was her pedigree. That woman had been owned by CoBos since she was born, and there he was making her IMC's queen." Po'Boy shook his head. "Went against the grain, and you know it did. You probably had your own version of those same kinda conversations here."

"You ain't lyin'. I hated that man for our Penny at first." Ace lifted an eyebrow as if to say, "So?"

"That changed when I got to know her. She's as true as they come, and it's not that she's shifted families, because she still loves the CoBos, but anyone can see that

Twisted has her loyalty, through and through. And that's as it should be. She just brought the two organizations a lil closer together, which is a good thing in and of itself, ya know?" Po'Boy nodded and lifted his beer. "Same thing's happenin' with me and Wrench. I know it, he knows it."

"And I know it," Ace said as Po'Boy took a drink. "But boy, you been IMC since you first straddled a bike. You've been the keeper of their skeletons in the closet for a time now. You sayin' you can leave that behind without any conflicts?"

"Yup." He nodded, keeping his expression carefully neutral. "I will not turn on them. Let me be crystal about that. But me holding my tongue about things that happened in the past? That ain't a divided loyalty. That's the basis of loyalty and should prove my worth even more."

"Be that as it may, why should my men trust you'd have their backs if anything came down on us?" Ace stomped the floor three times and set his empty on the table. He pointed a finger at Po'Boy's beer. "Finish that, the scrub'll be in here in a minute with fresh."

Po'Boy tilted it up, killing the bottle, and reached over to place it near Ace's. They were quiet as the door opened and the prospect came in, beer held in each hand. This time he placed one in front of Ace, then Po'Boy, before gathering the empties and leaving, again closing the door behind him.

"That's freaky as shit, man." Po'Boy glared at the doorway, listening hard. "Man a mute?"

Ace laughed. "No, he's just wary. Like I told you, your reputation precedes you." He angled in the seat, slinging an arm over the back of his chair. "Down to brass tacks, Po'Boy. Is this you asking if we'd take you as a patch?"

He stared at Ace for a moment before he nodded slowly. "It is."

"You and Wrench, this a long-term thing?" Ace surprised him by asking so directly. "Forget that gal, this something you're in for real?"

"Can't set her aside, man. We're a three-pete package deal these days." Po'Boy turned down the corners of his mouth. "You love your wife?"

"Ayeap. No second thoughts there. She's it for me."

"Wrench and Crissy are that for me. Same. I can't imagine my days without them, and if you won't have me and I have to go naked to be with him, I will. I won't put IMC at risk, but by the same token, I won't put him at risk, either. He needs me to wear blacks without even a support patch, I'll do it." He sat straighter, alert to every nuance of body language from Ace, holding his breath. He might be ready to do whatever was needed, including have nothing to do with either club, but never in a million years had he actually thought it would come to that. "He's it for me."

"In that case," Ace drawled the words slowly, then smiled big, head shaking side to side, "when you're ready to drop the IMC patch, we'll bring you in as a non-voting member. Keeps you out of prospect territory, which I suspect would be hell on earth for all of us, but keeps you from influencing club politics or business for at least a year. We'll put the full-member piece to an officer vote at the end of twelve months."

Po'Boy pulled in a shaky breath, hating that his reaction exposed so much of his hidden fears to this man. "Fuck."

"Damn, boy. You shoulda known how this would go." Ace stood and walked to where Po'Boy sat. He crouched down, putting himself at a disadvantage for a moment, head below Po'Boy's shoulders. "You know that boy's like a son to me. I love him. I wanted something for him. Something good. What you're building with that gal ain't what I expected, but as long as he says it's good, I can get behind it." He gripped Po'Boy's arm tightly. "Be that for him. Be good to him. All I can ask, brother."

"With everything I have, brother," purposefully using the phrase, Po'Boy responded quickly and gave a firm nod. "With everything I have."

Over the first few minutes of his ride home, Po'Boy let the certainty that everything would work out settle over him, then with a loud whoop, he gunned the throttle, weaving through traffic like a madman.

Wrench's bike was parked behind Crissy's car in the drive, and Po'Boy took a moment to study the house as he angled back into his spot.

Home. This was more than just a convenient place to stay, more than a temporary room across the lake, this was the building where he hoped to spend the rest of his life with the two people he loved more than anything else. He slung a leg over and stood, long legs eating up the distance to the door as he hurried inside.

"Honeys, I'm home."

Chapter Nine
Ty

Crissy had propped her feet in his lap, and was seated sideways on the couch. They were watching some TV show he didn't give a shit about, but she wanted company and he didn't mind being that for her. Also didn't mind touching what he could reach of her, especially when she moaned so sweetly as his rubbing fingers found a tender spot. She sat up slightly and looked at the front door just as Ty heard Lewis' bike roar once then fall silent.

"Do you know where he went today?" She tipped her head to look at him, hair swinging alongside her cheek. He shook his head. "He left early, and then I fielded two calls from Twisted for him. I guess he wasn't picking up."

Ty narrowed his eyes and turned back to the door as the handle twisted, Lewis stepping inside with a broad smile on his face. "Honeys, I'm home." Ty lifted a hand and Lewis angled to look at them, the smile growing brighter. "Hey."

"Hey, yourself." Ty resumed rubbing Crissy's feet, smoothing over her skin with his thumb, digging deep behind her toes, nails today painted a bright red that was sexy as fuck. "You have a good day?'

Lewis nodded, striding past and into their bedroom. He called back, voice distant and pitched to carry, "Yeah, I had a good one. Did you?" The thump of his boots hitting the floor rattled the boards under Ty's feet, and a moment later, Lewis walked back out, pulling on a clean tee. His fingers tugged the hem past his defined abdominal muscles, soft skin of his belly on display for a flashing moment that caught at Ty's breath. "Y'all got any ideas for supper?" He settled on the floor between Ty's knees and leaned his head back next to Crissy's feet, looking at Ty upside-down. "Hey, baby." He held out a hand and Crissy threaded her fingers through. "Babies."

"I've got some leftover soup I can heat up." Lewis groaned and threatened to bite her feet, bony teeth clacking near her toes. "Stop, it's healthy. You guys eat like animals most of the time. You could do with something that doesn't come out of a box." He gripped the side of her foot between his teeth and growled. Crissy shrieked and laughed. "Stop, stop. You made your point, brute." Ty chuckled at her put-on anger, happy to see that even when she tried, she couldn't hide her smile. "But, I might have the fixin's for a gumbo, if you'd prefer."

"I do prefer." Lewis pressed a kiss to her fingertips as she tried to shove his face to one side. "I can help cook, darlin'. You got the fixin's, I can do the prep work. I chop some mean celery." With the back of his skull pressed into Ty's groin, Lewis seemed to ignore the hardening cock under his head as he looked towards Crissy. "Love you, darlin'."

Her expression softened, that sweet, secret smile curving one corner of her mouth. "Love you, too. I have a call with Bob and Missy in half an hour. I can meet you in the kitchen afterwards, if you'd really like to help."

"How are they doing?" She hadn't spoken of her brother-in-law recently. Most of her stories surrounded her beloved niece. The pair lived with Bob's parents in Minnesota, their move precipitating Crissy's journey to Louisiana and into Ty and Lewis' lives. Crissy had stayed with her sister's family until Rhoda's death from cancer, and then afterwards to help ease Bob and Missy's burden. Now, she'd been in Louisiana for long enough it was time to think about a visit, one direction or another. Ty hoped Bob would bring Missy down south, so they'd get a chance to meet these people so important to Crissy. "He given any more thought to comin' for a visit? We got a spare room we can put him in, and there's the smaller bedroom that would be perfect for Missy."

"Or a nursery." From how Lewis froze after uttering those words, Ty would bet money he hadn't intended them to slip out. Crissy was staring at him with an open mouth, and Ty studied the man's face intently.

"Is that something you want, Lewis?" Crissy had regained control of her voice quicker than Ty and asked the question beating at his brain. "You've never really talked about kids."

"Ain't none of us have." Lewis shrugged and turned to face the TV, angling his face away. "It wouldn't take much to fix that room up for little Missy. You let me know if Bob's up for the trip, and I'll get on that." Ty and Crissy shared a look, and without speaking or needing to coordinate their movements, they both slipped from the couch to sit on either side of Lewis on the floor. "Fuck." Lewis dropped his head backwards onto the couch cushions. "It ain't nothing, you two. What show's this?" He snagged the remote from the coffee table and thumbed the volume up, and up, and up.

Ty plucked it from his hand and kept his finger on the button to turn the device down, until the sound was a quiet murmur. "It's something. And it's new. You really think you can drop a bomb like that and not have us tackle you to the ground to talk about it? Damn, Lewis. It's like you don't even know us at all." Ty snorted a laugh. "Crissy mine, what do you think? You think Lewis is lookin' for rugrats soonish or this a long-term plan?"

"I dunno, lover mine. How about you? Do you want kiddos? You haven't said anything, either." His gut clenched at the question, but he ignored that reaction. Crissy's laughter rolled just under the surface of her words, and Ty loved that sound more than anything. "And no one's asked my pithy opinion, either."

"You want kids?" Ty and Lewis spoke at the same time, Crissy laughing at both of them.

"I do." She spoke quietly, confidently, and when Ty leaned around Lewis to look at her, she held his gaze steadily. "I really do." She smiled, the expression radiant on her face. "I didn't know how much I'd like my Missy Prissy until she wormed her little way into my heart. She was the light of my sister's life, and after Rhoda died, she became the light of mine. If that's the kind of joy that a child can bring to a grieving house, then I imagine what would happen here, where there's so much happiness and love, and just the thought of it makes me happy."

Lewis leaned back on Ty's shoulder, hand out to Crissy. She crawled towards him, nesting into his lap and draping herself across Ty's legs. He wrapped his arms around them both, unsure what he was protecting them from, but it was an instinct he didn't try to dissect. Something profound was happening here right now, and he wanted to hold them all together.

"How does that work with us?" Ty knew it wasn't something he could approach like a bulldozer, but he had to ask. "I've watched the little ones growing up around the club, cousins havin' babies, friends doing the same, and you can see the legacy being made. Would you pick one of us and the other be an uncle or something?" That also set a churn up in his belly he didn't understand. "I've never given a great deal of thought to it."

"I have." Lewis' words were soft, velvet-smooth, and Ty could feel how still he'd gone, holding Crissy and being held by Ty. "Even back when we were just startin' out, I wondered what it would feel like to build a family with the two of you. I could be daddy, and Ty could be papa, and Crissy, you my love, would be our pretty, pretty momma."

"We can't both be the father." Ty chided him for dreaming the impossible. "That's now how biology works."

"Any child we have would be blessed with two fathers, Ty." Crissy lifted her head from Lewis' shoulder and gazed up at him. "Would it matter how it happened? The mechanics?" She pushed upright and twisted to look between their faces, an expression of dawning horror on her features. "Would it be a thing that came between you?" Head shaking, she started trembling. "If so, then we finish this little chat and I'll go make supper, and we'll never talk about it again. I love you." Her palm caressed Lewis' face, then Ty's cheek. "I'd never hurt you intentionally."

"It wouldn't matter to me, sweetheart." Lewis' arms bunched as he gave her a squeeze. "But I'm further along the path of thought than either of you. We can table the discussion for...fuck, indefinitely. No reason to upset the applecart over a bunch of coulda conversations." His neck twisted and he pressed a kiss to Ty's jaw, lips and teeth moving along his skin as Ty arched his neck to give better access. "Supper sounds like a good bet about now. I need to feel productive."

Lewis lifted Crissy and set her on the couch, then rose to a knee and kissed her before he stood, feet firmly planted between Ty's widely spread legs. Broad hands clasped both sides of his head and Lewis pressed a firm kiss along his hairline. "So much fuckin' love here. We're already blessed."

Chapter Ten

Lewis

Fuck.

Lewis tugged on a drawer pull, bringing out a cutting board and selection of knives. On autopilot, he retrieved the vegetables Crissy would need for the gumbo and rinsed them in the sink. His little mental slip had caused a tsunami of potential trouble. The instant the words were out of his mouth he was already kicking his own ass, because it wasn't what he'd been about to say at all. *I'm a fucking idiot*. Bowls handy to toss the chopped and diced veggies into, he started his portion of supper preparation, using slow, controlled breathing to calm his swirling mind.

As the scent of crisp, fresh vegetables began to fill the air, his stomach rumbled loudly and he chuckled at himself. Gumbo was good and satisfying. But it wouldn't be enough for him, and probably not Ty. He had his head stuck in the refrigerator, digging through the meat drawer, when a hand fell on the small of his back. Fingers tucked around his belt and firmly tugged him backwards. "My chef arrives, and I find myself unprepared."

He was surprised when he turned, and it was Ty standing behind him, not Crissy. "Or, my sous chef arrives, and he's less prepared than I am."

Without preamble, Ty grabbed the back of Lewis' neck and pulled him close, kissing him hard. Lewis opened his mouth, taking in everything Ty would give him, running hot within seconds, cock already blood-gorged and thumping at the zipper of his jeans. Unexpected didn't come close to covering it, and he rocked back on a foot to brace himself. Ty worked his mouth expertly, teeth and tongue competing for Lewis' avid attention, only to find that the movement of Ty's lips against his were mesmerizing, too.

Fingers in his hair wrenched his head back, breaking the kiss and Ty immediately applied the same attention to his jaw, then neck, focused on his Adam's apple. Ty's nose nudged the collar of his shirt to the side and he threatened with teeth, biting hard enough to sting just when fingers found Lewis' cock through his jeans, gripping and stroking.

A dark laugh, there were deep chuckles rumbling through Ty as he lurched forwards, pressing against Lewis. "Fuck, that's cold. What the hell is in your hands?"

Lewis blinked at the ceiling, centering himself, having been driven to distraction by Ty's attention. "I dunno." He huffed out a breath as the grip on his hair released and he brought his chin down. "I don't remember. Jesus, does it really matter? Fuck me, that was goddamned hot, baby. You hungry for more than supper?"

"I came in here to talk to you, but your ass was in the air, and then all I could fuckin' think about was bending you over the counter."

Lewis brought his hands to his belt buckle and laughed, because he had an onion in one, and links of boudin sausage in the other. "Here's the chill you felt." He shook his head. "Supper first, baby, then you can bend me over anything you want."

"I still get to watch," Crissy called from the living room, laughing musically. "Oh, nothing, Bob. How's Missy doing…" Her voice trailed off as she headed to the office for her video call.

"Supper," he told Ty. Bringing his chin down to his neck, he offered up what he hoped was a sly smile and held Ty's gaze for a second. "Then we can give our Crissy a show."

He turned back to the sink to hold the onion under water while he cut it into chunks, then finished dicing it on a fresh plate, before he took the casing off the sausage. "Baby, I need a couple of eggs, and can you see if we got any bread crumbs? I can use flour and cornmeal if I have to, but bread crumbs work best."

Ty rummaged around for a minute and set the requested items on the counter. "What's that gonna be? Thought we were having gumbo?" He shifted things to one side and set a bowl down. "I'll make a batch of cornbread. Hot buttered cornbread always goes with everything."

"Boudin balls. Just fried sausage, nothing special. Like cornbread, it goes with just about everything."

The murmur of Crissy's voice rose and fell in the distance while the two men worked side by side comfortably, economy of movement showing the kitchen was familiar ground for both of them. It took a few minutes, but Lewis realized the silence had gotten heavy, stifling, and when he glanced at Ty, he saw tension in the set of his jaw, muscles clenching in bunches as he gritted his teeth.

"What's up?" He'd moved on to preparing a yellow mustard potato salad, something his stepfather's cook had always made to go alongside gumbo. Once in a while, Lewis would put it as a base in his bowl instead of rice, depending on the kind of dish made. "You got somewhat to say, just say it. No judgment in these walls." He paused as he rinsed his hands, emphatically shaking droplets of water away as he ended with, "Ever."

Ty shot him a glance over his shoulder as he turned to the stove. The hot oil in the skillet was ready for his dropped spoonfuls of cornmeal mix. "Kids." Head tipped down, he stared at the popping circles of yellow, surrounded by bubbles as it fried fast in the pan. "Crissy told me it didn't matter, after you left the room, you know? She said we would always be enough." His eyes darted to the side again, glancing off Lewis and back to the skillet. "Was a lie, though."

"Yeah, you see her face when she said she wanted 'em?" Lewis smiled. "Beauty, so much beauty there when a woman's thinking about carrying life shared with the people she loves. She lit up like a roman candle."

"I wanna give her that." Ty's confession wasn't surprising, and neither was his next statement. "But I don't have that drive."

"Got no cravin' to see a little mix of Ty and Crissy runnin' around? We could call 'em Tissy." He chuckled. "Or Cry, that'd work too."

"Lissy or Crew wouldn't sound bad." Ty laughed softly, sounding sad.

Lewis fit himself against Ty's back, wrapping his arms around his middle and holding tight. "Why's that a bad thing, Ty?"

"I dunno. It just feels sudden." Ty shook his head, drifts of his hair brushing against the side of Lewis' face. "Like out of the blue tonight, and it's a big fuckin' deal, deciding to bring another life into the world. Seems like it would be more talk and less 'let's do this thing' to me."

"So, it's sudden for you." He shrugged. "Just means you aren't at the same place she and I might be. Doesn't make it a bad thing, either way. We're not ahead of you, or behind you, just on a different timeline, maybe." He gave Ty's ribs a squeeze. "The idea of her pregnant with your baby, that makes me fuckin' giddy. Your eyes in a kid's face topping her smile? That'd be absolute beauty right there." He slipped one hand down and cupped Ty's belly as if he were a woman. "Her carryin' my child under her heart? Spending her life and love and energy growing my baby, gettin' to feel it grow and move and become its own self, protected safe inside its momma? That's magic of the highest order. I'd be ready tonight, she wanted to start, but only if it fit your image of what we're making." He rubbed a circle on Ty's belly, then dipped his hand down and scraped his nails across Ty's thudding, hard dick. "This says there's something in there you liked, baby." He gave another light scrape, then kissed Ty's neck as he glanced at the skillet. "Better turn those over, you're gonna burn 'em."

Ty took a deep breath at the warning and flipped his cakes, then reached down and pressed Lewis' hand tight to his crotch, hips rocking against the pressure. "You make a compellin' case for the idea."

"No decisions made, nor do they have to be made now...but at some point, not making a decision is makin' one, you know?" Lewis gave Ty's cock a squeeze as he pressed his own dick against Ty's ass, smiling against his neck when Ty seemed torn between thrusting forwards or back. "I gotta get my shit rollin'. I'll make the roux, and then I'll get the oil goin' for the rest of it."

Forty-five minutes later, Crissy floated in, an expression of profound happiness on her face as she danced to where Ty was setting out bowls and plates. "Guess what, guess what?" She draped herself on his shoulder, pulling him around to face her. Chin lifted, she rolled up on her toes to press a smiling kiss to his lips. "Guess, guess!"

"Uh, you found your favorite socks?" Ty glanced at Lewis. "You got anything better?"

"Yeah," Lewis said, putting the cover back on the dutch oven he had the gumbo in. "You found my favorite vibe and got it chargin' up for me." He waggled his eyebrows at her as Crissy laughed. "Vibe beats socks, hands down."

"*Bob's coming to visit*." She squealed and did a pirouette, coming to rest facing Ty again so she could lift to her toes and kiss him a second time. "And he's bringing my Missy Prissy."

"That is great news, honey." Ty wrapped his arms around her shoulders and pulled her close. Lewis took the three strides to put himself at her back and bracketed her with his body, hand around the back of Ty's neck to hold tightly. "I can't wait to meet both of them."

"Oh!" Crissy's head came up and she nearly clocked Lewis on the chin, making him jerk back, and Ty laugh. "There's so much to do."

"When are they comin'?" Lewis looked at the calendar on the front of the refrigerator, important job dates marked for Crissy, and club events for him and Ty.

"Two weeks." Her answer was a sigh and her shoulders fell slightly. "That's the date that worked best for both of us."

"Works for all of us, honey." There was a span of days where nothing was marked, and the visit would fall in the midst of that. "How long can they stay? You want as much time as you can get, right? Not a quick trip?"

"I talked him into a full week." She burrowed her face against Ty's chest. "I wanted more, but I'll take what I can get."

"A week's a good span of time." Ty's voice was husky, and Lewis looked up to see his eyes shining. "It'll be good for you to be with the little girl, your niece." He swallowed, and Lewis wondered what was going on. Ty wasn't usually the emotional one, that role fell to Lewis more often than not. "I can't wait to meet them, either."

"Supper's ready," Lewis reminded them and gave both a squeeze before he stepped away. "We got quite the spread, so fill a plate and let's eat in the living room tonight. Watch the rest of that show or whatever."

"You just wanna cuddle on the couch," Crissy accused him, taking a bowl from his hand and moving to the gumbo pot. "I feel bad I didn't help."

"We had it covered." Ty laughed. "Don't get to be men grown and not learn how to cook a lick or two."

"Well, this—" Crissy plucked a piece of sausage out of the gumbo and popped it into her mouth, then made a show out of sucking the sauce off her fingers. "—is finger-licking good."

Chapter Eleven

Ty

Lying in bed with Crissy as they waited on Lewis to finish up in the bathroom, Ty idly ran a finger along her chest, between her breasts and down to her tummy. He circled her belly button with a light touch until it irritated her and she swatted his hand away with a scold of, "Tickles."

With his fingertips, he dragged up the hem of her sleepshirt, finally making his way to bare skin. She shifted beside him and spread her legs slightly, inviting him to go farther if he wanted.

Oh, yeah. I want.

He flattened his hand against her hipbone, found the edge of her panties and slipped underneath. Smooth skin, then the rough tease of hair, and then that glorious, slippery, creamy wetness just waiting for his touch. His breath hitched in his chest at the knowledge that this was his. All this—from the calm time in the kitchen with Lewis, to the snuggling and touching on the couch, and now the aroused partner at his side—all of this was his.

Ty played to the soundtrack of Crissy's sighs and soft moans, to the indrawn sips of surprise when he delved deep, fingers sliding into her effortlessly. His thumb strumming across her clit brought her hips upwards in a thrust as if she were a marionette and he controlled her strings. Palming her sex, he fit two fingers inside her entrance and circled the opening, around and around, until she huffed out a frustrated sound. He bypassed her pussy and dipped to her ass, circling and pressing until her hips shoved downwards, chasing his touch.

Sliding down the mattress, he took the covers with him as he stripped her panties from her legs. She pressed her knees together while Ty shed his boxer briefs, kneeling at her feet naked. "Lose the shirt, too, honey." Palm on her belly, he felt her muscles tense and shift as she removed it over her head, hair tousled and wild on the pillow. As beautiful as she was in this moment, he imagined the expression on her face from earlier and a deep longing to give her whatever she needed struck him like lightning. *She wants a baby.* Ty slipped a hand between her knees, spreading her wide for him.

131

Certainty filled his chest with warmth and a broad dash of eagerness. *She gets a baby*.

Timing would have to be right, and like Lewis had said earlier, that didn't have to be decided upon right now.

No, right this moment he got to love on his woman, knowing their man would join them in a few minutes, and be surprised and pleased at what he'd find in their bed.

He was sprawled off the end of the mattress, legs dangling as he ate her hard and fast. Still in that position when Lewis strolled into the room, an entrance marked by his dark chuckle and a long, drawn-out "Daaammmn." Mouth on her clit, lips pursed and sucking, Ty had his thumb deep into her pussy, his middle finger thrusting in and out of her ass in time with his attack on that delicate bundle of nerves.

"Lewis," she cried out, and Ty tilted his head to look up her body. Breasts clutched in each hand, her head was thrust back against the pillows as she soared higher and higher. Ty drew a knee underneath him, angling his ass up into the air in as open an invitation as Crissy had given him earlier. Lewis' fingers drew a line of fire along the back of his thigh, up and up, until he gripped the ramrod hard cock dangling between Ty's legs. Lewis gave it a twisty stroke that made Ty's toes curl.

"I do believe I found my way to the right place—" A wet, hot stripe was laid up one ass cheek, and Ty clenched in anticipation. "—to sate myself fully." Hands on Ty's cock and balls, stroking and rolling, pulling and tugging, Lewis burrowed his face between Ty's cheeks until he could tongue his hole. A mind-numbing bliss stole over him, and Ty closed his eyes, fixated on the sensations Lewis was dragging out of him. A heavy buzz landed on the base of his spine with every lash of Lewis' tongue, every wiggling dive inside, timed with another twist and tug on the head of his dick.

Ty came back to himself with Crissy's hand in his hair tugging his face against her as she reared up, legs tensing around his shoulders. "Please," she called out, "Lewis, Ty," and he redoubled his efforts, settling his chest on the mattress as he arched his back for Lewis.

Touch against him slowed, eased back, and Lewis gave a wet, smacking kiss to his ass before Ty lost the heat of him altogether. Rustling came from off to the side, the crinkle of plastic and then the click of a tube that was unmistakable.

Lewis crowded in beside him on the end of the bed, pressing Crissy's knee wider to give him access. "Lemme have her ass, baby. Gonna rev her right up." Crissy had bought a basketful of toys weeks ago, and they'd used a few of the tamer ones. *Looks like Lewis is digging deep tonight*. Ty drew his finger out, twisting his hand around to pull up on her pussy with his thumb. Her hips tilted, and he saw a flash of purple as Lewis slipped something between her cheeks. A click followed by a buzz had her fingers twisting harder in his hair, a soft cry set free on the air of the room. "Awww, yeah. Our Crissy girl likes that assplay. That's butt plug number one for the night."

"Number one?" Ty lifted up and got a lungful of musky air, surrounded by the scent of an aroused Crissy and Lewis fresh from the shower, masculine bodywash mixing with her smells in a mouthwatering way.

"Ummm hmmm," Lewis hummed, disappearing again. "Continue on, Ty. Make our Crissy feel good, baby." Another crinkle of plastic and snap of the lube top had him clenching his ass cheeks hard. Then Lewis' mouth was back on him, hand on his cock taking long, hard pulls that would have him on the edge in minutes. A chill touched his skin, then something thin pressed against the ring of muscles around his hole. He bore down as Lewis had coached so many times, head snapping up when it slipped easily inside, Lewis' efforts and the lube making the glide natural and easy. He felt full as the plug prodded gently, withdrawing slightly and then thrusting forwards, and then he stiffened because glowing sparkles had appeared around the edges of his vision, telling him Lewis had found his magic button. "Awww, yeah." A click, but instead of a buzz like Crissy's toy, he was hit with an irregular thudding against his prostate.

"Oh, my God," he breathed, chin lifting as his head arced up. "That's...Jesus." The plug shifted and clicked, and the thuds came in different intensities now, hard and slow then a beat of nothing followed by fast and light. *Fucking hell*. It was too much and not enough, all rolled up into one, and he groaned. Lewis' hair brushed the underside of his neck, then Ty heard the soft sounds of his mouth on Crissy's pussy. *This is too…* "Lewis, I can't."

"I know, lover," Lewis said, a broad river of desire in his roughened voice. "God, I know. You crawl up there next to our Crissy, get on your back, get some pressure on it and work that thang. Make it your bitch. I'll get my playtime from here."

He did, cock arrowed straight up at the ceiling when he rolled over, hips rising and falling as he found an angle and rhythm. He reached down to find the hard, plastic base wedged between his cheeks and gave it a tentative tug, finding it was snug, in no danger of falling out. *Okay.* Pressing against it with two fingers as he rocked up caused the sensation to become less intense. He held it there for a moment, then pushed the base down, lifting the tip of the device inside him and immediately saw the blinding white of stars, clutching at the sheets with his other hand.

Heat hit his cock, followed by a light squeeze. When he glanced down, he saw Crissy had stretched out a hand, her thumb sliding across the tip where a steady flow of fluid streamed from the slit. Lewis reached up and put his hand over hers, the increased pressure and heat ratcheting up the level of Ty's arousal even more.

His head dropped back with a thud. *It's too much.* "God, Lewis." He lifted his head again, looking farther down their bodies to where Lewis was sprawled at the bottom of the bed, a wide grin on his face as he played with Crissy's pussy, the hum of the toy in her ass now going up and down in volume as he teased with the intensity. "There's…"

"I know, baby. I know. Let it seep into you. Find your pace and follow it. Nothing you do is wrong, always remember that. It's all pleasure, and we're all in this together. You get yours, and we all love it." Lewis' arm moved, stroking fingers into Crissy's channel. One of her knees was propped over his shoulder, and he dropped his face back to her pussy, tongue flashing as he lapped at her.

Ty let his head fall back, losing himself to the sensations of his lovers' hands moving on him, the plug pounding on his gland, the wash of cool air across his overheated skin. Sweat beaded on his chest and he swiped at it with one hand, fingernails pausing in a rough scratch across one nipple. Grip back on the base of the plug, he played, pushing it deeper and tugging it back, wiggling it to find the best angle, heels dug into the mattress to give himself leverage.

Crissy cried out beside him, the tone in her rising wail one he knew, and he turned his head to watch her come. Lewis was on his knees in an instant to cover her, and the mattress jostled, bed creaking with a timeless song of sex and love and Ty watched his body move and roll as he fucked her through and past her orgasm.

Dick still pointed straight up, impossibly hard and rigid, he palmed himself as he played with the plug, riding the edge of climax himself. Lewis yanked at her hips roughly, elbowing Ty's leg as he lifted Crissy, pounding into her hard. His mouth was drawn into a thin line across his face, sweat falling from the tips of his hair to her belly when he leaned over her for leverage.

Lewis fell back abruptly as he pulled out of Crissy, then he bent forwards across both of them and stripped his cock furiously, hand blurring with the speed of his punishing strokes. Hard and fast, the wet sound set Ty's nerves raging again, knowing what he'd taste if he could just get his mouth on Lewis right now. Tang and sweet of Crissy's juices mixed with the musk and spice of Lewis. He jammed his fingers against the base of the plug, shoved it against his prostate hard and held it there as he came with Crissy's hand on his cock, pulling and tugging, drawing out ropes of white shooting in an arc that covered his belly. He angled his hips to splash the next stream on her, and then Lewis came with a shout, showering both of them with strings of hot, white fluid.

Ty scrabbled around the edge of the toy with his fingernails, desperate to turn it off, to get it out, because even though he'd come, ejecting copious amounts of spunk, his cock was still thumping and he was done, exhausted, and needed to be lying like a ragdoll on the bed, not drawn up in a bow by the...fingers slipped over his, nudging him aside, and there was a click followed by blessed stillness inside him. The removal of the toy left him feeling empty in a way he'd never experienced, and he looked at Crissy when she laughed at him. "Wha?" He sounded drunk to his own ears, slurring even those few syllables.

"You sounded like me." Then she made a noise, and he saw Lewis walking away from the bed, purple and black plugs in his hands. "That's how I feel when you guys pull out after we're done. Fulfilled, but..."

"Not really sad, just, missing something now. Right?" She nodded. "I love you, Crissy girl. You want a baby, we'll make a baby." Her face lit up, and he knew this was right. Knew it down to his bones. *No matter what, we're all in it. This is our forever.* "The three of us, we'll rock the shit out of parenthood."

Chapter Twelve

Lewis

He stood in the doorway for a moment, taking in the sweet scene playing out on the bed right now. Ty had cuddled into Crissy, a wadded bunch of fabric beside the bed evidence of him trying to clean up after he'd taken two loads on his belly. Lewis refolded the wet rag in his hands, conserving the heat from the water for a moment. Ty needed this opportunity to connect with Crissy on this topic so he could move past it. They'd had a chance to talk in the living room, and had, but Ty processed things differently from either of them.

Crissy went on her emotions, her gut feeling, and she was seldom wrong. It was what had allowed him to sweep her up when they met, because she'd decided that being with him was worth exploring. And it had given him this triad, since she'd done the same when offered the opportunity to discover what it was like to be loved on by two men.

Lewis knew he was an overthinker. Still, after his talk with Ace, it hadn't taken long for him to realize he'd already been mulling the idea over. Maybe he could blame Yousa's pregnancy for making this seem a goal within reach, but whatever the genesis, the outcome was the same. He wanted to see Crissy bear their children. His or Ty's, the paternity didn't matter to him. Just as long as whatever children they were graced with, had her smile.

Ty was a mixture of both decision methods, moving from gut reactions for intense situations, and dealing with the long-term strategy that came with politics in the club. It was in his raising, and Lewis couldn't fault him either way. He understood. The problem was, once he jumped one way, like he had earlier, Lewis had expected it would take him longer to find his way back to center. *Happy to be wrong*.

"Y'all want a lick and a promise of a washup, or wanna jump in the shower quick, rinse off the sticky?" He showed them the rag in his hands, and Crissy voted by spreading her legs for him. Warmth bloomed in his chest at her confidence and trust, and his voice was rough when he told her, "I gotchu, sweetheart." He climbed onto the bed from the side, placing Crissy between him and Ty and swiped at her belly and breasts first, then Ty's belly, before moving down to gently wash her sex. "Need a little cleanin', baby?" he asked Ty, who nodded and lay compliant as Lewis shifted around to reach his ass. That sweet, sweet ass that had taken Ty to heights of pleasure tonight Lewis hadn't expected. Getting out the plugs was a whim, one he'd known Crissy would be in tune with, but Ty's reaction was so much more than he could have hoped. "Was good, yeah?" *Fuck, where'd that come from?* It wasn't like him to be unsure of himself like that.

"You know it was good, Lewis." Ty's soft chide was delivered with a smile. "I can't imagine how good it'll be like when you're in there for real."

He turned his back on the duo and Lewis schooled his features carefully before he tossed the rag and turned around. *Fuck.* "Gonna be so good." That, right there, was where his fears lay.

Crissy rolled to her stomach, arms thrust under the pillow as she rustled around and got comfortable. Ty fit himself to one side of her, his arm curled around her ribs. Lewis bent over them to kiss Ty, earning a soft grumble as the man had to reposition himself for the caress, then getting some slow, sleepy tongue action, which was what he'd wanted all along.

He lay at Crissy's other side, trailing his fingers down her spine, curving his touch around Ty's arm back to her skin. Down, then up, idle touches that grounded him more than anything else, drowning out the voices from his childhood that shouted he'd never been enough, called him white trash, screamed that he was a gay boy, a fa— His brain stuttered and he breathed through the remembered pain. They were unwelcome and harmful things he'd left in the dust, but like all bad memories had a way of doing, could circle back around and smack him in the gut, leaving him feeling like shit for days.

"What's goin' on in that head of yours?" Ty's tired eyes blinked at him over the curve of Crissy's shoulder. She was out, sleeping sweetly, cocked up on one hip to lean against Ty's side. "Stay, Lewis. Don't leave and go somewhere to stew all night again."

Lewis shook his head. "I won't. I'll sleep in a bit. Just got some things caught in my mind I need to put to rest first."

"I liked what we did tonight." Ty's eyes slid closed, and when they opened again, he looked more alert. "Liked that shit a lot more than I'd have thought. If you'd described it to me, I'd have given it a hard pass, but right there, it turned me inside out, man. It was crazy how good it was."

"You want more, you think?" Dangerous questions given his own insecurities, but Lewis had never been afraid of digging around in the dark until he found what he needed. This was just another snipe hunt. "I'm happy with how things are now, but it was nice to have you be the monkey in the middle for a while tonight. Give you all the lovin' you can stand."

Ty snorted softly, hand moving up to rest on Crissy's scapula, shifting out of the way of Lewis' quiet trailing fingers. "Monkey in the middle is about right. Train this monkey," he snorted again. "You always know what to do."

There it was. An opening he couldn't have crafted any better if he'd tried, but Lewis shied away. "Heard what you said to Crissy about babies."

"Another place where you knew what to do. I just had to take a minute and breathe, think it through. It's a lifelong thing, making a family. My mom and daddy showed me that every decision impacting folks other than yourself have to be considered carefully. Making a new being, that's a big fuckin' decision." Ty's hand came down on Lewis', halting his movement so Ty could twine his fingers through, holding on. "It's the right decision. And you knew it. As always."

Fuck. If Ty was going to keep throwing that out there, maybe it was time for Lewis to come clean about his secret.

He yawned big, jaw cracking with the strain as he settled farther into the mattress, relaxing, the release of sleep finally circling close. "Well, that's two things tonight you've given me credit for that I don't have a bit of experience in." He chuckled, giving Ty's fingers a squeeze from where he lay on the pillow next to Crissy. Lewis closed his eyes, took a deep breath, and confessed, "I've never made a baby. And I've never fucked a man."

The bed shifted, and Ty's voice was close to him when he asked, voice rising at the end, "What the fuck?"

Lewis smiled, surrendered his tension on a sigh, and fell asleep.

FINI

THANK YOU SO MUCH FOR READING
SHELTER MY HEART!

I truly hoped you enjoyed this story in the NTNT MC world. Thanks for taking this trip along with me and a couple of my favorite boys. Next up is Retro's story in *Trapped by Fate on Reckless Roads*, and I hope you'll give him a listen, too.

~ML

ABOUT THE AUTHOR

Raised in the south, *Wall Street Journal* & *USA TODAY* bestselling author MariaLisa learned about the magic of books at an early age. Every summer, she would spend hours in the local library, devouring books of every genre. Self-described as a book-a-holic, she says "I've always loved to read, but then I discovered writing, and found I adored that, too. For reading...if nothing else is available, I've been known to read the back of the cereal box."

Want sneak peeks into what she's working on, or to chat with other readers about her books? Join the Facebook group! **bit.ly/deMora-FB-group**

deMora's got a spam-free newsletter list she'd love to have you join, too: **bit.ly/mldemora-newsletter**

RECIPES FROM THE STORY

Crissy's Chicken and Andouille Gumbo

Ingredients

- 1/2 cup each unsalted butter and all-purpose flour
- 1 tablespoon canola oil
- 1/2 cup each chopped bell pepper and onion
- 1/4 cup each chopped celery and carrot
- 2 cups each chopped andouille sausage, and shredded roast chicken
- 3 cups chicken broth
- 1 tablespoon Creole spices*
- 2 teaspoons filé powder
- 2 cups raw long grain white rice

Preparation

- Takes about an hour and 15 minutes to prepare, once you have everything chopped and ready.
- In a small cast-iron pan over medium heat, melt butter. Add flour, and whisk vigorously until combined. Cook, stirring frequently, until a brown roux forms, about 15 minutes. Remove from heat, and set aside.
- Cook rice over low heat, cover, and set aside.

- In a large Dutch oven over medium-high heat, add canola oil. Add bell pepper, onion, celery, and carrot, and cook stirring frequently, until tender, about 5 minutes. Add sausage, and cook until lightly browned. Add roux, and stir to combine. Slowly whisk in broth, and cook, stirring occasionally, until mixture begins to boil. Stir in chicken, Cajun seasoning, and filé, and serve immediately over fork-fluffed rice.

Ty's Cornbread

Ingredients
- 1 cup cornmeal
- 1 teaspoon each salt and white sugar
- 1 tablespoon shortening
- 3/4 cup boiling water
- Enough oil or bacon fat to cook

Preparation

- Quick dish, you can start this 15 minutes before serving.
- In a medium bowl, combine cornmeal, salt, and sugar. Add boiling water and shortening; stir until shortening melts.
- Pour oil or bacon fat to a depth of 1/2 inch in a large skillet and heat until popping.

- Shape cornmeal mixture into flattened balls using a heaping tablespoon as a measuring guide, drop into hot oil. Cook on each side until done, with crispy brown edges. Serve hot with butter.

Lewis' Fried Boudin Balls

Ingredients
- 2 or 3 links Cajun-style boudin sausage, about 12 ounces
- 1/2 sweet onion diced
- 1/2 cup each all-purpose flour and seasoned fine dry bread crumbs
- 2 large eggs (well beaten)
- Enough oil for deep-frying
- Creole spices to taste.
- Heat the oil in a deep fryer to about 360F to 370F

Preparation

- About 45 minutes from start to finish.
- Remove boudin from casings and crumble. Shape the boudin into 1 1/2-inch balls. The heat from your hands will help hold them together. If they stick, moisten your hands slightly.

- Fill one small bowl with flour, another with eggs, and a third with breadcrumbs (mixed with creole spices, if desired).
- Coat each ball with flour, then coat with the beaten egg, then gently roll in the bread crumbs to cover thoroughly. You may need to rinse your hands several times in hot water while rolling the balls. (I just like saying balls a lot.)
- Fry the balls, two at a time, in the hot oil until golden brown.
- Serve with a good remoulade sauce or with Creole-style mustard.

Lewis' Potato Salad

Ingredients
- 2 pounds russet potatoes peeled and cubed (4-5 decent sized taters should do it)
- 1 1/2 teaspoons salt
- 5 large eggs hard-boiled, peeled and smashed lightly with a fork
- 1/2 cup celery diced
- 1 small Vidalia onion minced
- 1/2 cup dill pickle relish, plus 2 Tablespoons juice
- 2 1/2 tablespoons prepared yellow mustard (or creole style for extra pizzazz)
- 1/2 cup mayonnaise
- Salt and pepper to taste

Preparation

- Takes about 45 minutes, but leave time for the salad to cool.
- Boil potatoes in lightly salted water until falling apart, about 10 minutes. Drain, and return to hot pan to dry.
- Combine potatoes, eggs, celery, onion, pickle relish and juice in large mixing bowl.
- Add half mustard and mayonnaise and stir thoroughly.
- Add remaining mixture for consistency, careful not to make the potato salad too watery.
- Salt and pepper to taste.
- Refrigerate until ready to serve. Is actually better on day two after the flavors mix all together.
- Can garnish with whatever, paprika if you have it, chopped green onions, jalapenos if you've made it spicy.

Creole Spices

Want to make your own creole spices? Easy 'nuff:

- Combine a quarter teaspoon each of onion powder and garlic powder. Add a dash or more of oregano, basil, thyme, black pepper, white pepper, cayenne pepper, and paprika. Salt to taste.

Also by MariaLisa deMora

Alace Sweets

A dark thriller, this book is not a light read. Filled with edge-of-your-seat suspense, this intense story commands the reader's attention as it drives towards the explosive ending. Alace Sweets is a vigilante serial killer, with everything that implies and is sure to trip all your triggers. Be ready.

At seventeen, Alace Sweets turned a corner in her life, taking the wrong shortcut home from school.

Resisting the harsh knowledge her attackers will never be made to pay for their actions, Alace takes a stand. Justice must be served, and if fate's scales are out of balance, she's determined to set things right as best she can.

When the laws of men fail, the rules of Alace prevail.

5-Star Reviews for Alace Sweets

"Whatever deep dark trench [deMora] pulled a character like Alace from should be revisited again and often."
~Confessions of a Serial Reader

"deMora has a superb story-line and exceptional character development. All of her characters have such depth that will intrigue the reader..."
~Turning Another Page

"Hot, sweet, dark thriller."
~Beth D

"It will keep you on the edge of your seat and give you chills."
~Escape Reality Book Blog

"Disturbing, haunting, sickly; yet hot, sexy and heart racing!"
~Amanda L

"From the first page [deMora] pulls you into the world she has created and you do not even try to escape..."
~Little Shop of Readers Blog

"A must read for all those dark, gritty romance fans out there."
~Sweet & Spicy Reads

"You will find yourself so drawn into the story that the outside world is blocked out and your locking the doors and turning on all the lights."
~Danena F

"Don't judge me for bonding with a vigilante serial killer, she's more than what she does."
~iScream Books

"Thrilling...chilling...full of suspense, nail biting edge of your seat excitement."
~Tracey H

"Every time MariaLisa deMora picks up her pen (or opens her computer), she creates characters you want to believe in."
~Gail S

"Intriguing dark storyline, beautiful love story and nail-biting conclusion, what more could a reader ask for?"
~Manda M

"This book takes you a dark and twisted ride that is gripping..."
~Renee Entress' Blog

"This book is dark and gritty and I literally had to take a day off from reading it because it's that intense."
~My Girlfriend's Couch

"This is my favourite book so far from this author ... I recommend this book if you enjoy dark romantic thrillers."
~Cheekypee Reads and Reviews

"There's not enough stars to give this book and 5 just doesn't really do it justice!"
~DeLane C

"I couldn't put this book down from page one! Tried to stop & go to bed but couldn't sleep thinking about Alace and got up & finished the book."
~Debbie M

"MariaLisa DeMora, wordsmith that she is, made this a story of the enlightenment of a woman and finding love in a life where she has had none."
~Kat W

Hard Focus

This is an intense page-turner, a gut-punch twist-filled story about a woman who has confidence in herself, believes she's a good judge of character, and has filled her life with people she can trust. She's right, but she's also very, very wrong. Readers will have a time of it trying to decide who to watch closest.

Where do you place your trust when your own instincts betray you?

Connie Rowe is a receptionist at a respected legal firm. She's a little bit sassy, a lotta bit happy, has good friends, and is adored by her neighbors.

Life is good.

She's got a boyfriend she enjoys spending time with. He can be a little intense, but he's got a lot going on in his own life, sorting out his young daughter and nightmare of an ex.

Life is grand.

"Trust your gut." That's what Connie's police officer father told her often, training his daughter to believe in herself through the years.

But … what happens when you can't? When your intuition lies?

What happens when things come into Hard Focus?

5-Star Reviews for Hard Focus

"Hard Focus is one very well-written tale. 5 stars is not enough for me."
~Tabitha

"What a powerful story. [deMora] kept me invested from the first word to the last."
~Jesse R

"[deMora] has a certain magical touch to writing her characters, that they become either your nemesis, your best friend, or your love interest. That is certainly portrayed in this spin around. Loved it, loved it, loved it."
~Sandy K

"I strongly recommend this book for both entertainment and to broaden your knowledge of certain laws that must be revisited."
~Words Turn Me On

"A intense page turner. Once you start, you can't put the book down."
~Tracey H

"A beautifully written, powerful read that I can't rate highly enough. This story will stay with me always."
~Gayle

"This book had twists I didn't see coming. Loved it!"
~Lori R

"Wow! I am in awe of deMora's skill in crafting this story."
~Kat W

"I keep sayin that there just aren't enough stars to give to some of Marialisa deMora's books...this one is no different!"
~DeLane

"Where do I start with this one...I read this in 3 1/2 hours uninterrupted, I absolutely could NOT put it down. Very deep, keeps you guessing, what's gonna happen next, kind of book. I love how strong her characters are, especially the females!"
~Wendy I

"Sometimes I feel like MariaLisa deMora is the one I should be watching out for. I started reading her books because I'm addicted to MC Romance, but then she decides to change things up and I just follow her wherever she leads me like a Pied Piper. I never know what to expect ... but it's always an adventure."
~Rosa for iScream Books Blog

"A plot full of twists and turns, a story that's not quite what it seems, strong characterization, jaw dropping revelations... what more do you need from a book?"
~Manda M

"This book kept me turning the pages wondering what was going to happen. I am usually pretty good at guessing twists but not with this book. She totally surprised me and brought me out of my funk. 5 stars."
~Glenna M

"What an amazing story! Filled with a smidge of suspense, a dash of action and a heap of realism of our country's laws and how their vague application to victims can adversely affect its citizens and the people in their lives."
~Naughty Mom Story Time

ADDITIONAL SERIES AND BOOKS

Please note that books in a series frequently feature characters from additional books within that series. If series books are read out of order, readers will twig to spoilers for the other books, so going back to read the skipped titles won't have the same angsty reveals.

Rebel Wayfarers MC series:

Mica, #1
A Sweet & Merry Christmas, #1.5
Slate, #2
Bear, #3
Jase, #4

Gunny, #5
Mason, #6
Hoss, #7
Harddrive Holidays, #7.5
Duck, #8
Biker Chick Campout, #8.5
Watcher, #9
A Kiss to Keep You, #9.25
Gun Totin' Annie, #9.5
Secret Santa, #9.75
Bones, #10
Gunny's Pups, #10.25
Never Settle, #10.5
Not Even A Mouse, #10.75
Fury, #11
Christmas Doings, #11.25
Gypsy's Lady, #11.5
Cassie, #12
Road Runner's Ride, #12.5

Occupy Yourself band series:

Born Into Trouble, #1
Grace In Motion, #2 (TBD)
What They Say, #3 (TBD)

Neither This, Nor That MC series:

This Is the Route Of Twisted Pain, #1
Treading the Traitor's Path: Out Bad, #2
Shelter My Heart, #3
Trapped by Fate on Reckless Roads, #4
Thunderstruck, #5

Rebel Wayfarers & Incoherent MC (NTNT) crossover stories:

> *Going Down Easy*
> *No Man's Land*

Mayhan Bucklers MC series:

> *Most Rikki-Tik*, #1
> *Mad Minute*, #2
> *Pucker Factor,* #3
> *Boocoo Dinky Dau,* #4 (TBD)

Borderline Freaks MC series:

> *Service and Sacrifice*, #1
> *More Than Enough*, #2
> *Lack of Inbetween,* #3
> *See You in Valhalla*, #4

If You Could Change One Thing: Tangled Fates Stories

> *There Are Limits*, #1
> *Rules Are Rules*, #2
> *The Gray Zone*, #3

With My Whole Heart series:

> *With My Whole Heart*, #1
> *Bet On Us*, #2

Alace Sweets series:

> *Alace Sweets*, #1

Seeking Worthy Pursuits, #2

Other Books:

Hard Focus
Dirty Bitches MC: Season 3

More information available at **mldemora.com**.